BREATH

TIM WINTON

PICADOR

First published 2008 by Hamish Hamilton,
an imprint of Penguin Group (Australia)

First published in Great Britain 2008 by Picador

This edition first published 2009 by Picador
an imprint of Pan Macmillan Ltd
Pan Macmillan, 20 New Wharf Road, London N1 9RR
Basingstoke and Oxford
Associated companies throughout the world
www.panmacmillan.com

ISBN 978-0-330-45572-5

3 5 7 9 8 6 4 2

A CIP catalogue record for this book is available from
the British Library.

Printed in the UK by CPI Mackays, Chatham ME5 8TD

Breath

TIM WINTON was born in Perth in 1960
and is the author of novels, collections of stories,
non-fiction and books for children. He has
won the Miles Franklin Award three times,
and been twice shortlisted for the Booker Prize,
for *The Riders* (1995) and *Dirt Music* (2002).

Also by Tim Winton

Novels

An Open Swimmer

Shallows

That Eye, the Sky

In the Winter Dark

Cloudstreet

The Riders

Dirt Music

Stories

Scission

Minimum of Two

The Turning

for Howard Willis

WE COME SWEEPING up the tree-lined boulevard with siren and lights and when the GPS urges us to make the next left we take it so fast that all the gear slams and sways inside the vehicle. I don't say a thing. Down the dark suburban street I can see the house lit like a cruise ship.

Got it, she says before I can point it out.

Feel free to slow down.

Making you nervous, Bruce?

Something like that, I murmur.

But the fact is I feel brilliant. This is when I feel good, when the nerve-ends are singing, the gut tight with anticipation. It's been a long, slow shift and there's never been any love lost between Jodie and me. At handover I walked up on a conversation I wasn't supposed to hear. But that was hours ago. Now I'm alert and tingly with dread. Bring it on.

At the call address Jodie kills the siren and wheels around to reverse up the steep drive. She's amped, I guess, and a bit puffed up with a sense of her own competence. Not a bad kid, just green. She doesn't know it but I've got daughters her age.

When she hits the handbrake and calls in our arrival at the job I jump out and rip the side door back to grab the resus kit. Beneath the porch steps on the dewy grass is a middle-aged bloke hugging himself in silence and I can see in a moment that although he's probably done his collarbone he's not our man. So I leave him to Jodie and go on up to announce myself in the open doorway.

In the livingroom two teenage girls hunch at opposite ends of a leather couch.

Upstairs? I ask.

One of them points without even lifting her head, and already I know that this job's become a pack and carry. Usually they see the uniform and light up with hope, but neither of them gives me as much as a glance.

The bedroom in question isn't hard to find. A little mat of vomit in the hall. Splinters of wood. I step over the broken-down door and see the mother at the bed where the boy is laid out, and as I quietly introduce myself I take it all in. The room smells of pot and urine and disinfectant and it's clear that she's cut him down and dressed him and tidied everything up.

I slip in beside her and do the business but the kid's been gone a while. He looks about seventeen. There are ligature marks on his neck and older bruises around them. Even while I'm going through the motions she strokes the boy's dark, curly hair. A nice-looking kid. She's washed him. He smells of Pears soap and freshly laundered clothes. I ask for her name and for her son's, and she tells me that she's June and the boy's name is Aaron.

I'm sorry, June, I murmur, but he's passed away.

I know that.

You found him a while ago. Before you called.

She says nothing.

June, I'm not the police.

They're already on their way.

Can I open the wardrobe? I ask as Jodie steps into the doorway.

I'd prefer that you didn't, says June.

Okay. But you know that the police will.

Do they have to?

The mother looks at me properly for the first time. She's a handsome woman in her forties with short, dark hair and arty pendant earrings, and I can imagine that an hour ago, when her lipstick and her life were still intact, she'd have been erect and confident, even a little haughty.

It's their job, June.

You seem to have made some kind of . . . assumption.

June, I say, glancing up at Jodie. Let's just say I've seen a few things in my time. Honestly, I couldn't begin to tell you.

Then you'll tell me how this happened, why he's donc this to himsclf.

I've called for another car, says Jodie.

Yeah, good, I mutter. June, this is Jodie. She's my partner tonight.

Go ahead and tell me why.

Because your husband's broken his collarbone, says Jodie. He broke down the door here, right?

So what do I tell them? the mother asks, ignoring Jodie altogether.

That's really for you to decide, I say. But there's no shame in the truth. It's fairer on everybody.

The woman looks at me again. I squat in front of her beside the bed. She smooths the skirt down onto her knees.

I must be transparent, she murmurs.

I try to give her a kindly smile but my face feels stiff. Behind her I can see the usual posters on the wall: surfers, rockstars, women in provocative poses. The bookshelf above the desk has its sports trophies and souvenirs from Bali and the computer goes through a screensaver cycle of the twin towers endlessly falling. She reaches for my hand and I give it to her. She feels no warmer than her dead son.

No one will understand.

No, I say. Probably not.

You're a father.

Yes, I am.

Car doors slam in the street below.

June, would you like a moment alone with Aaron before the police come in?

I've had my moment, she says, letting go my hand to pat her hair abstractedly.

Jodie? Will you just pop down and let the police know where we are?

Jodie folds her arms petulantly but goes with a flick of her little blonde ponytail.

That girl doesn't like you.

No, not much.

So what do I do?

I can't advise you, June.

I've got other children to consider.

Yes.

And a husband.

He will have to go to hospital, I'm afraid.

Lucky him.

I get to my feet and collect my kit. She stands and brushes her skirt down and gazes back at the boy on the bed.

Is there anyone else you'd like me to call?

Jodie and two cops appear at the door.

Call? says June. You can call my son back. As you can see, he's not listening to his mother.

When we're almost back to the depot for knock-off Jodie breaks the silence.

So when were you planning to let me know what all that was about?

All what?

With that poor woman. For a moment there I thought you were flirting with her.

Well, you can add that to your list of complaints.

Look, I'm sorry.

Arrogant, aloof, sexist, bad communicator, gung-ho. Obviously I missed a few things, coming in late. But for the record, Jodie, I'm not a Vietnam vet. Believe it or not I'm not old enough.

I feel awful, alright?

So get a roster change. Be my guest. But don't do your bitching at handover in the middle of the bloody shed with your back to the door. It's unfriendly and it's unprofessional.

Look, I said I was sorry.

When I look across at her I see in the lights of a passing truck that she's almost in tears. She hangs onto the wheel as though it's all that's holding her together.

You okay?

She nods. I roll a window down. The city smells of wet lawns and exhaust fumes.

I didn't think it would hit me that hard.

What?

That was my first suicide, she murmurs.

Yeah, it's tough. But it wasn't suicide.

Jesus, Bruce, they had to bust in the door and cut him down. The kid hanged himself.

Accidentally.

And how the hell do you know?

I'm a know-all. Remember?

She grimaces and I laugh.

God, you're a strange man.

So I gather.

You're not gonna tell me, are you? I can't believe you won't tell me.

I sit there a minute and think of those poor bastards sanitizing the scene before we showed up. The mother sitting there, trying to choose one shame over another. The other kids downstairs cold with shock. The father out on the grass like a statue.

Maybe another time, I say.

Well, she says. I rest my case.

We ride back to the shed in silence.

I hurtle on too long through the pounding submarine mist. End over end in my caul of bubbles until the turbulence is gone and I'm hanging limp in a faint green light while all the heat ebbs from my chest and the life begins to leach out of me. And then a white flash from above. Someone at the surface, swimming down. Someone to pull me up, drag me clear, blow air into me hot as blood. He spears down and stops short and I recognize my own face peering through the gloom, hesitating an arm's length away, as if uncertain of how to proceed. My own mouth opens. A chain of shining bubbles leaks forth but I do not understand.

So I wake with a grunt on the sofa in the empty flat where afternoon sun pours through the sliding door. Still in uniform. The place smells of sweat and butter chicken. I get up, crack the door and smell the briny southerly. I take a piss, put the kettle on and snatch the didj up off the seagrass matting of the floor. Out on the balcony my herbs are green and upright. I tamp down the beeswax around the pipe mouth and clear my throat. Then I blow until it burns. I blow at the brutalist condos that stand between me and the beach. I blow at the gulls eating pizza down in the carpark and the wind goes through me in cycles, hot and droning and defiant. Hot at the pale sky. Hot at the flat, bright world outside.

I GREW UP in a weatherboard house in a mill town and like everyone else there I learnt to swim in the river. The sea was miles away but during big autumn swells a salty vapour drifted up the valley at the height of the treetops, and at night I lay awake as distant waves pummelled the shore. The earth beneath us seemed to hum. I used to get out of bed and lie on the karri floorboards and feel the rumble in my skull. There was a soothing monotony in the sound. It sang in every joist of the house, in my very bones, and during winter storms it began to sound more like artillery than mere water. I thought of the Blitz and my mother's stories of all-night bombing raids, how she came up out of the ground with her parents to find entire streets gone. Some winter mornings I turned on the radio at breakfast half expecting to hear the news that whole slabs of the district had been lost to the sea – fences, roads, forest and pasture – all chewed off like so much cake.

My father was afraid of the sea and my mother

seemed indifferent to it and in this they were typical of the place. It was the way most locals were when I was a boy, and they were equally anxious or ambivalent about the forest around us. In Sawyer you kept to the mill, the town, the river. On Sundays blokes from the sawmill liked to row all the way down to the broad shallows of the inlet to fish for whiting and flathead and my father went with them. I can't even remember who owned those long, heavy dories moored to stakes near the riverbank – they always seemed rather municipal – and whoever climbed in first became oarsman and skipper. The trip downstream could take an hour or more, especially if you stopped at snags and sloughs to try for bream. On rare mornings when the bar was open and the sea flat, a few boats ventured out to catch snapper, but the old boy would never leave the shelter of the estuary and no one, man or boy, could shame him into going further.

He began to take me along when I was seven. I liked the creak of the oars in their rowlocks, the disembodied shadows of pelicans rushing over the mottled flats. The big wooden dories held three or four men each, and it was quiet out there with them on the water. The other men were always tired and hungover, but my old man was just naturally subdued. When any of them spoke up they had the barking tone of the industrial deaf. They had fags-and-sawdust coughs, those men. Their jungle hats stank of prawns and fishblood. They were bachelors and returned soldiers and bank-beaten farmers who seemed oddly solicitous of my father even if they did mock him for his teetotal ways. He was a greengrocer's boy from a village in Kent who never told me stories about his old life. But he was no mystery to his workmates. He was, simply put, a steady hand and as far as I could see this was all they required of him.

We fished with handlines and sinkers moulded from lead roof-flashing, and while we filled hessian sacks and wiped slime and scales off on the scarred wooden thwarts, the surf bumped the high, white levee of the bar. Manes of spray hung above the rivermouth and flagged back in the breeze. When the bite was slow and I grew bored and restless, the old man consented to row me across to where I could get out and climb up onto the sandy wall and watch the great seas roll in.

I was a lone child and solitary by nature. Somewhere along the way I became aware that my parents were old people with codgers' interests. They pottered about with their vegetables and poultry. They smoked their own fish and mended and embroidered. Of an evening they listened to the radio, or the wireless, as they called it. Although they weren't quite grandparent age, they were definitely of a different order to the parents of other kids, and I felt that their singularity marked me out somehow. I felt protective of them, even if I was, in truth, a little embarrassed. Like them I didn't care much for football or cricket. I avoided teams of any kind and the prospect of organized sport was a misery. I did like to hike and climb but it was only in swimming that I really excelled and this must have been quite a surprise to my emigrant parents, neither of whom could swim to save themselves.

At the first signs of spring giving way to summer townie kids gathered after school near the bridge at the riverbank to dive off the crude springboard. The river was brown with tannin and cold as hell but it was very slow-flowing and safe to swim in. It was there that Loonie and I became friends.

Ivan Loon was twelve and a whole year older than me. He was the publican's son and although we'd been at school together half our lives we never had the remotest thing in common. That is, before we realized that we'd each independently perfected the art of causing riverside panic.

One November afternoon I coasted down to the river on my bike to have a jump off the plank but when I got there four girls and somebody's mother were slithering up and down the bank, yanking at their own ears and screaming that there was a boy in the water, that he was drowning right beneath them. Naturally they didn't know *which* boy because they were from out of town, but they knew he was *a* boy for he'd been there a minute ago and simply hadn't come up from a dive and were there sharks and couldn't I for God's sake stop asking questions and just get on with doing something.

Sun blazed down in rods through the big old gums. There were dragonflies in the air above us. I saw a towel near the diving plank and beside it a grubby pair of thongs, so I had no reason to doubt there was a crisis. Only the sluggish water seemed harmless and these females, who were making a frightful noise, looked so strangely out of place. I should have twigged. But I went into action on their behalf. As I bolted out to the sagging end of the springboard the wood was hot and familiar underfoot. I looked down at the wind-ruffled surface of the river and tried to think. I decided that it would be best to wade in from the bank, to work my way out by feel, and just keep diving and groping in the hope of touching something human. There wasn't time to go looking for help. I was it. I felt myself rise to the moment – put-upon but taller all of a sudden – and before I could embark upon my mission, or even pull my shirt off, Ivan Loon burst from the water. He came up so close to shore with such a feral shriek the woman fell back on the mud as if shot.

I stood bouncing on the plank while she lay in the muck. Then she reared up on her elbows. Loonie started to laugh, which didn't really help her mood. I had never in my life seen a woman so angry. She charged into the water, lunging and swiping to no avail, while Loonie just ducked and feinted and giggled. He was a freckly sort of kid but he went so red with pleasure and exertion all his freckles disappeared. The poor woman never got close to him. Her frock ballooned about her. She made tanty noises like a toddler. Loonie sculled himself out of range, bobbed provocatively for a bit, then stroked off to the shadows of the far bank. Left alone with her once again, I realized it was more fun to pull this prank than it was to stand by while someone else did it. I began to feel more guilt than glee. Two Dr Scholl's sandals floated upstream in the breeze and I watched until I could bear it no longer and dived dutifully after them. As I snared them and sidestroked back to the bank they clunked together like firewood. It was embarrassing to see this grown woman standing there in her clinging dress with her dimpled knees and chubby legs all muddy.

There's tree roots down there, I told her. You just dive down and hold on. It's easy.

She never said a thing, just snatched her shoes and scrambled back to the girls higher up the bank, and while I lay in the water trying to decide how to feel about her she smoothed herself back into some kind of authority and led the others up through the trees and out of sight. I felt sympathy and contempt all at once. Car doors slammed and there was the stammer of a starter motor.

Easy, is it? said a voice hot and close in my ear.

I jerked aside with a shout. Loonie bawled with laughter.

Brucie Pike, he said. You're all talk.

Am not.

Are so.

Am not.

Well, then, Pikelet, you better prove it.

So I showed him what I had. We dived all the rest of that day, kicking down time and again to the opaque depths of the Sawyer River to hold our breaths so long that our heads were full of stars, and when we finally climbed out, spent and queasy, the bank plunged and canted beneath us in the evening twilight. That was the first of many such days and we were friends and rivals from then on. It was the beginning of something. We scared people, pushing each other harder and further until often as not we scared ourselves.

MY PARENTS didn't quite approve of Loonie. He was a mouthy urchin who roamed the town at will. He lived at the pub and my oldies were not pub-going folk. The fact that Mrs Loon was not Loonie's actual mother seemed to cause Mum some discomfort, but she tried not to let on. My parents were discreet and kindly people. Loonie seemed to provoke more anxiety in them than antipathy. They were so quiet and orderly that only a few years after they were both dead and buried few Sawyer locals could remember much about them, whereas Loonie was a creature of an entirely different sort. Now and again you'll still run into someone in Perth or Kuta with a story about Loonie's old antics, and although the tales are almost always apocryphal they still bear the essential elements of his wildness. Someone as solitary and feral as he was could naturally be expected to be a little simple and naïve but Loonie was neither. At twelve he was more worldly than either of my parents and in a queer way they were intimidated by him. He started out patronizing them. He was amused by their innocence, by their English clothes and the brogues they wore in the garden. He mimicked the old man's pottering walk and chafed his hands the way my mother did. Before I ever thought to bring him over to our place he began turning up of his own accord. He appeared at the front fence like a stray, just hanging about at the end of the long, rutted drive, a restless figure seeming to await or even silently demand an invitation to cross the cow paddock. When he was in our yard or, later, at the lunch table, the old folks were nervous and diffident. He batted his big green eyes and joshed them gently in his loaded, mocking tone, smiling until his sun-split lower lip bled against his teeth.

After a week or two, having made an effort to disguise his reluctance, the old boy finally consented to my bringing Loonie out in the boat with us. Loonie was so jovial that first time, so full of larks and noises of appreciation, that he gave us all a headache and even I thought it an act of mercy on the old man's part to have him back again. I think he saw how dearly Loonie loved it, how eager he was to help, how keen he was to please. Despite their primness I think my parents recognized some greater loneliness in my new friend, and they sensed that for all his derisory swagger he respected and even loved them in his way. He often crouched alongside my father at the smoker while the fish were racked and he was forever seizing a teatowel whenever he found himself in my mother's kitchen. Early that summer, when we fell in together without discussion, he was at our place most of the day and into the evening. He always overstayed, yet somehow knew to leave before someone finally dropped a hint.

On Sundays we fished the inlet with the mill men and in late December, when the holidays arrived, we spent weekdays at the river making picnickers nervous. We salvaged junk from the tip so we could augment our bikes with weirdly extended forks and handlebars. We tilted our banana seats and sissy bars until we were virtually riding uphill on any gradient. Out on the highway Loonie played chicken with log trucks while I hid in the bracken at the edge of the forest, willing him to desist and urging him on all at once. We had escape tracks that wound back through the regrowth and spoil ground toward town, so that by the time a rattled truckie pulled over and backed up laboriously, we were long gone. It was a boyhood that now seems so far away I can understand why people doubt such days ever existed. If you tried to talk about it you'd be howled down as some kind of nostalgia freak, called a liar before you even got started. So I don't discuss it much. In this I suppose I am my father's son, a bad communicator, a closed book. I've bored people in bars and lost a marriage to silence. I don't want to join anybody's misery club, to be adopted as a fellow victim of whatever syndrome is doing the rounds this week. I'll talk if no one's listening. It's like blowing the didjeridu, cycling air through and through, doing little more than explaining yourself to your self while you're still sane enough to do it. I'm not a nostalgic man. I can go for weeks without thinking about my boyhood and Sawyer and Loonie, but in my line of work you're going to see things like tonight's asphyxiation and get a cold feeling you're not likely to explain to some kid in a crisp new uniform, someone who's already decided that you're a piece of work.

AS A BOY in Sawyer I yearned to swim in the ocean but the old man was firmly against it. If I asked him on fishing days he refused on the grounds that I would need watching and this meant he'd have to leave the boat and his lines and his workmates on his only day off and it was too much to ask of him. I knew deep down he'd have gladly sacrificed an hour for my pleasure if only he'd been able to swim enough to save me if I got into strife, but his impotence was beyond admitting. When I asked if I could just ride out to the rivermouth with Loonie he shook his head. Too rough, too far, no way. But I wanted to swim where I could see the bottom, to be where those long, creaming breakers trundled in from the south so I could dive down and see them pass overhead. I hankered after the sea as I'd never done for anything else before. I'd always been such a compliant, respectful child and until that point I was usually content. But being denied access to the ocean was intolerable. Even without Loonie's influence,

I would probably have defied the old man in time – I figured I was almost a teenager, after all – but that summer I was emboldened by my new friend's indifference to authority, and though I asked and begged and pleaded beforehand, I eventually set out with Loonie one Saturday and rode to the coast without my father's blessing. It began with a lie. I said we were headed for the river but as we coasted through town and past the servo we simply doubled back behind the pub.

You know why it is, Loonie said as we rolled down the turnoff. You know why your old man's scared, don't you?

Yeah, I said after too long a pause. I didn't want to talk about the fact that my father couldn't swim. I wasn't that disloyal yet.

You're lyin, Pikelet.

I stood on my pedals, wary of being seen by someone from the mill.

Snowy Muir, said Loonie.

Who's he?

Bloke from the mill. Fishin off the Point when they opened the bar. All the snapper was runnin. King wave got him. Just ran up the rock and hauled him in. Found him three days later out at the Holes.

The stony bitumen made my teeth chatter. Wattlebirds buzzed us from the thicket edges.

And your old boy was there, Pikelet. He saw him go.

When was this? I asked, trying to sound sceptical.

1965.

How . . . how do *you* know?

I live at the pub, you dick. Only thing flows faster'n beer is talk.

It bothered me not to have known this precious detail about my father. I rode on in silence.

We freewheeled downhill a mile or so until we came to the long, flat stretch where the estuary meandered into shoals on our left and the boggy horse paddocks opposite rose to steep timbered hills. The sun was on our shoulders and already, over the whirr and clatter of our bikes, you could hear the ocean.

On the last uphill stretch a flatbed truck wallowed off the saltpan onto the tar ahead of us. Without a word, Loonie put on a spurt and chased it. There were people on the back of the truck who laughed and cheered as he caught up and grabbed onto the tie-rail. The old banger went up through the gears, making speed against the incline. Loonie and his bike drew away and I saw the pink flash of his face as he looked triumphantly back across his shoulder. I doubt the driver even knew Loonie was there, clinging on gamely in the rear, but they surged uphill, leaving me in their wake, until all I could hear was the whining diff and the faint sound of laughter. Eventually speed and one-handedness got the better of Loonie who got the wobbles and let go. He veered wildly onto the gravel edge and was gone through the reeds, a rippling commotion like a blast of wind, and the last thing I saw was the bike shooting riderless from the vegetation before it somersaulted into the shallows.

By the time I finally ground my way up to the crest of the hill Loonie and his crumpled machine were loaded on the bed of the idling truck and the driver seemed to be waiting for me. When I drew alongside I saw that although his knees were stripped and his shirt was in tatters Loonie looked insanely happy. He mugged and winced for the benefit of a girl who looked sixteen and had flowers painted on her jeans. Beside the pair of them was a stack of surfboards and a three-legged dog. From the cab, three blokes with tumbleweed hair told me to climb up, and so we rode like that to the headland until the bitumen gave way to a dirt track that we bounced down through peppermints and wattles to the hard white beach and the overpowering roar of surf.

The blokes piled out of the cab, snatched up their boards and were gone before either of us could climb down or thank them, so we thanked the girl instead. She shrugged and wriggled her toes in the sand. The dog plugged around in circles, competing with Loonie for her attention.

From the granite headland whose rocks were daubed with warnings about the dangerous current, the beach stretched east for miles. We watched the surfers plunge into a churning rip alongside the rocks and from there they shot out toward the break. Waves ground around the headland, line upon line of them, smooth and turquoise, reeling across the bay to spend themselves in a final mauling rush against the bar at the rivermouth. The air seethed with noise and salt; I was giddy with it.

Loonie had a nice old limp from his prang but it didn't prevent him from clambering out across the rocks with me and the girl and the three-legged-dog to watch the blokes glide by on their boards. They hooted and swooped and raced across the bay until they were like insects twitching in the distance. The girl, who said she was from Angelus, gave us apples from her woven bag. She talked about Iron Butterfly and plenty of other things I knew as little about and I don't know how I kept up my end of the conversation because my mind was firmly elsewhere. I couldn't take my eyes from those plumes of spray, the churning shards of light. Was this what the old man was afraid of? I tried to think of poor dead Snowy Muir but death was hard to imagine when you had these blokes dancing themselves across the bay with smiles on their faces and sun in their hair.

I couldn't have put words to it as a boy, but later I understood what seized my imagination that day. How strange it was to see men do something beautiful. Something pointless and elegant, as though nobody saw or cared. In Sawyer, a town of millers and loggers and dairy farmers, with one butcher and a rep from the rural bank beside the BP, men did solid, practical things, mostly with their hands. Perhaps a baker might have had a chance to make something as pretty as it was tasty, but our baker was a woman anyway, a person as dour and blunt as any boy's father and she baked loaves like housebricks. For style we had a couple of local footballers with a nice leap and a tidy torpedo punt, and I would concede that my father rowed a wooden boat as sweetly as I'd seen it done, in a manner that disguised and discounted all effort, but apart from that and those old coves with plastic teeth and necks like turtles who got pissed on Anzac Day and sang sad songs on the verandah of the Riverside before they passed out, there wasn't much room for beauty in the lives of our men. The only exception was the strange Yuri Orlov who carved lovely, old-world toys from stuff he fossicked up from the forest floor. But he didn't like to show his work. He was shy or careful and people said he was half mad anyway. When it came to blokes, his was all the useless beauty the town could manage.

For all those years when Loonie and I surfed together, having caught the bug that first morning at the Point, we never spoke about the business of beauty. We were mates but there were places our conversation simply couldn't go. There was never any doubt about the primary thrill of surfing, the huge body-rush we got flying down the line with the wind in our ears. We didn't know what endorphins were but we quickly understood how narcotic the feeling was, and how addictive it became; from day one I was stoned from just watching. We talked about skill and courage and luck – we shared all that, and in time we surfed to fool with death – but for me there was still the outlaw feeling of doing something graceful, as if dancing on water was the best and bravest thing a man could do.

We sat on the headland with the girl and the dog until the breeze turned and everyone paddled in. We rode into town on the back of their old Bedford, sunburnt and blissed to the gills.

The old man was furious – he saw the truck, caught sight of Loonie hauling his warped bike home and figured it out for himself – but nothing could touch me, no threat, no expression of disappointment, and certainly no gentle appeal to reason. I was hooked.

Loonie and I went back and back and back that summer. We hitched and rode and walked, begging boards from the Angelus crew when they paddled in for lunch or at day's end, and week by week we literally found our feet, wobbling in across the shorebreak, howling and grinning like maniacs. Even now, nearly forty years later, every time I see a kid pop to her feet, arms flailing, all milkteeth and shining skin, I'm there; I know her, and some spark of early promise returns to me like a moment of grace.

THE FIRST BOARDS we got were Coolites, short, boxy styrofoam things which squeaked when you touched them and blew wherever the wind wanted them to go. Because they had no fin they were all but impossible to steer, like a sailboat with neither keel nor rudder, but we thought they were the duck's nuts. Loonie pestered his stepmother into buying him one and I got mine second-hand from a farm kid who'd just returned from a holiday in Queensland that he'd hated. Those boards certainly made the ride out to the coast a fresh challenge. They were too wide to fit neatly under a boy's arm and so light that they lurched and twisted as though they were alive and trying to take flight. A good crosswind gust could put you and your bike into the roadside scrub in a moment. Our early efforts with them could hardly be called surfing. We were little more than animated flotsam. Then we shaped crude fins from plywood and set them into our boards with paraffin wax and everything changed; we had control, we could steer. At last, we were surfing.

That summer Loonie and I surfed until we were sun-cooked, until our arms gave out and the foam chafed our bellies raw. At night my mother dabbed Flavine on the stippled scabs on my chest and sponged vinegar down my sunburnt back. There was no hiding from her what I was doing but she said nothing about it. Whenever the old man found my Coolite propped on its end in his shed he tossed it out into the weeds without a word. I still helped him pluck poultry and turn dirt for the vegetable garden but we didn't fish much together anymore and I knew that he felt forsaken. I'd moved on from him, we both knew it, and try as he might he couldn't hide how much it hurt. He never mentioned the older boys who dropped me at the end of the drive some afternoons. I half expected him to interrogate me about them, but he seemed resigned. He'd always looked old but now he seemed fearful and disappointed. I was only going surfing, but to see his face you'd think I'd left home already.

In the new year Loonie moved across to the Ag School. It was the only junior high in the district and if you wanted to go on and finish the final two years you had to board in Angelus or take the dawn bus every day. That year, during school hours, Loonie and I began to live in slightly different worlds. By his account Ag School was strange and tough. In those days it was boys only and you learnt about wool and crops and insemination. There were fights out by the machinery shed nearly every Friday, and some evenings when he dropped by Loonie had bruises and scrapes all over him. He never backed away from anything or anyone; that was just how he was. He talked about kids who shaved, who had arms like Christmas hams, older blokes who said his mother was a slut, which was why he fought them. I was still a bit vague about what a slut actually was and I was confused about whether the references were aimed at his mother or his stepmother, so I didn't press him for clarification. In July, when Mrs Loon packed up and shot through in the middle of the night, Loonie seemed unmoved. I'd hardly known her. I remember a squat little woman with dark, curly hair and a gold tooth. He never spoke about her again.

Some winter weekends we rode out to the rivermouth with our Coolites, but often as not the swell was so big we never got beyond the thumping shorebreak and over at the Point the rip looked treacherous. Chastened by our failure Loonie and I would towel off and get dressed and scuttle out along the rocks to watch the Angelus crew confront the great, heaving waves that pivoted past the headland to spew into the bay. They sat way outside of where anybody normally surfed, so far off that their silhouettes were only intermittently visible. For long periods nobody did much out there but bob about, scratching seaward every few minutes to avoid the looming sets that threatened to bury them. In such a swell the rocks along the Point were awash so high up that we were forced back into the scrub to stay safe and dry. We hunkered down in our lookout, pulled our coats about ourselves and willed somebody to take off, until eventually one of the Angelus crew would turn and start to paddle. Some of the waves were as high as us in our nest on the headland. Whenever somebody sucked up the courage to go we were beside ourselves; we screamed and hooted for him as he clawed his way over the edge and we groaned and seized our hair when he came unstuck. There'd be a horrible ball of foam, a snarl of limbs, and a board shooting skyward to flip like a tossed penny above the carnage while we searched the water for a head or an upstretched hand. Thrilled and appalled, we could sit there for hours. It was our coliseum.

One surfer seemed to show up on only the very biggest days. He was quite an old guy and his board was so long and thick that he'd carry the thing on his head down through the peppermint scrub to the beach. Then he'd jog to the water and launch himself into the crunching shorebreak and aim straight for the rip, paddling on his knees, always as casual as you like, whatever the conditions. You'd barely see him for half an hour and then a set would break out wide, like a squall rolling into the bay, and you'd suddenly pick out the white squirt of a wake on the grey-brown crags of a wave big and ugly enough to make you shiver. There he would be, that tiny figure, strangely upright and nonchalant, rising and swooping until he was close enough to be more than just a silhouette. His skill was extraordinary. There was something special about his insouciance and the princely manner in which he cross-stepped along his long, old-timey board, how he stalled and feinted and then surged in spurts of acceleration across the shoaling banks, barely ahead of the growling beast at his back, and when the wave fattened toward the deep channel in the middle of the bay, he'd stand at the very tip of the board with his spine arched and his head thrown back as if he'd just finished singing an anthem that nobody else could hear.

Neither of us knew who this man was. We reckoned he must be from the city, but when Loonie piped up to ask the Angelus crew about him, they just grinned and ruffled his taffy hair, which made him so mad I had to drag him away before he started a fight I didn't want to be in.

WHEN IT WAS too stormy and vile to go out to the coast, Loonie and I stayed in town and entertained ourselves at the river, paddling bits of junk from bank to bank, leaping from trees, swinging on ropes. We had lungs like camel bladders by then; we sledged each other mercilessly, each daring the other to break the two-minute limit beneath the diving board. In the summer sea when it was flat-calm and there was nothing else to do but dive down and lie on the clean, ribbed bottom and hold our breaths to count Mississippis we got pretty close to our goal. But trying it at the bottom of the river in winter was another challenge altogether. It was a grim business down there in the dark, clinging to the saurian roots of rivergums, so cold that a minute's worth had us surfacing blue-lipped and dizzy. We climbed up onto the bank too numb and stunned to even feel the fire we'd left burning to warm ourselves by.

Loonie's old man found us shivering like that one drizzling Sunday afternoon in July.

Look at youse two stupid pricks, he muttered. It's rainin and the water's as cold as a witch's bits and you're bloody swimming.

We *like* swimming, said Loonie without even looking up.

Karl Loon had his flying jacket on, all leather and sheepfleece. Loonie said he'd been in the air force, though from what I could hear of his old man's faint accent it wasn't necessarily the kind of outfit that flew in English. Mr Loon was a big, square bloke with a boxy head. He might have been Polish once or maybe a Croat – you'd have to listen hard to hear it. The wool of his coat collar was as yellow as a nicotine stain. His hair was oiled and parted on the side and even though this was the first time I'd ever seen him in the outdoors, he always looked sunburnt.

And now you burnin green wood, he said. No wonder youse can't get warm.

We're orright, said Loonie sullenly.

Chop me some wood for the pub and I'll let youse

have some for here. What d'you reckon? I got five ton in just now and no one to split it.

Loonie hugged himself and shook his head.

Youse got something better to do?

We'll do it for money, said Loonie.

How much?

Ten bucks a ton.

His old man laughed.

Each! said Loonie.

You can git to buggery, said the publican, walking away.

But it turned out that we did split the wood, and we did the job for a fiver a ton each. We chopped in the rain for days out in the long yard behind the Riverside, amidst a wasteland of weeds and lines of washing, broken sofas and stone troughs. An old fella with a humpback and a drooping fag sat and watched us from beside the glittering ranks of empties as we split those sappy mill-ends and sucked at our splinters and stacked the cut wood in the lean-to by the pub laundry. Before we'd even finished our five tons we had offers of similar work all over town. Drinkers either took pity on us, or saw us as a means of getting the missus off their backs, but any way you looked at it, we were in business.

LOONIE LIKED anything with an edge on it. There were grindstones in some of the sheds where we worked, and he used them to sharpen our axes and the pocketknife he always carried. Whenever we took a break, when the lady of the house brought us mugs of tea and a few lamingtons, he'd want to play chicken. Most often we used the knife. We spread our hands on the pulpy chopping block, jabbing the blade faster and faster between our fingers – first looking and later blind – until one of us begged off or began to bleed. Some sheds had dartboards, so we played William Tell. A lamington, said Loonie, was just as good as an apple. He invented games involving axes and feet, axes and anything, really. Any game would do as long as it was dangerous.

At each perilous undertaking – and with Loonie there were plenty of them – he always volunteered to go first. For a while I thought it was about honour, that it was his way of taking responsibility for whatever stupid idea he'd come up with – something gentlemanly, perhaps, a mark of friendship – but eventually I saw that Loonie went first out of need; he was greedy about risk. He absolutely loved a dare. He would actually dare *you* to dare *him*. This wasn't optional. He required it of you, insisted on it. When it came to things like this he was completely compulsive. Being with him was like standing near a lethal electric current. The hairs on your arms literally stood up and you were afraid and mesmerized, always drawn to connect.

That winter we chopped enough wood to buy ourselves real surfboards. They were dinged-up and obsolete, the cast-offs of the Angelus crew or somebody's sister's boyfriend, but they were proper foam and fibreglass and they were tokens of our arrival. We scraped the hard, dirty wax from their decks and rubbed them down afresh. We stood them in the old man's shed to admire their leaf-like outlines and the sharky rake of their fins. The old man wasn't at all happy about the fact that I'd been working at the pub but he didn't toss the boards out into the weeds as he'd done with the Coolites. He'd seen the calluses and divots in my hands. He knew I'd earned that surfboard with a bent back and once again, after the longest time, I felt the distant glow of his respect.

ON A STILL morning in late September, in a lull between cold fronts, Loonie and I pedalled with our boards to the Point where the waves were small and clean and the cold water was as clear as the sky. We sat inside at the mellow edge of the rip and paddled into waist-high rollers that carried us hooting and howling in to the beach. We had the place to ourselves. The sandbanks rippled underfoot, schools of herring swerved and morphed as one in the channel, and across in the bay the breaths of breaching dolphins hung in the air.

I will always remember my first wave that morning. The smells of paraffin wax and brine and peppy scrub. The way the swell rose beneath me like a body drawing in air. How the wave drew me forward and I sprang to my feet, skating with the wind of momentum in my ears. I leant across the wall of upstanding water and the board came with me as though it was part of my body and mind. The blur of spray. The billion shards of light. I remember the solitary watching figure on the beach and the flash of Loonie's smile as I flew by; I was intoxicated. And though I've lived to be an old man with my own share of happiness for all the mess I made, I still judge every joyous moment, every victory and revelation against those few seconds of living.

We surfed until we were limp and when we floundered ashore the bloke I'd noticed before was waiting. He sat on the back of a cut-down Kombi with a red dog that sprang down to meet us.

Life on the ocean wave, eh boys? said the bloke with his board-bump knees drawn up to his beard.

My teeth were chattering and I couldn't speak but I nodded. I recognized him as the one who paddled out when the surf was huge, the man with the old-timey board.

You wouldn't be dead for quids, wouldja?

We just shook our heads in agreement and laughed and shuddered while the red dog danced circles around us. The bloke smiled as though we were the funniest sight he'd seen all year. He whistled the dog up and we bolted to where our clothes lay warmed from a day in the sun.

The Volkswagen hawked and sputtered to life. The bloke wheeled it around on the sand and looked at us a moment before offering us a lift. He waited, laughing, while we fumbled numbly with buttons and buckles.

We bounced up the track with the dog lapping at our salty ears. At the top of the hill where our bikes lay in the weeds, he pulled up and we climbed out, burning with pins and needles where the circulation had kicked back in.

You're a pair of hellmen, you two, he said through the cab window.

Why's that? said Loonie.

Surfin bareback in all weather. You're either stupid or broke.

Both, I said.

How old are you?

Thirteen, said Loonie.

Almost thirteen, I said, stretching things a bit.

The bloke had a mass of curly bleached hair and his beard was of the same stuff. He was a big man and muscular, with grey eyes. It was hard to tell his age but he had to be thirty or more and that made him a genuinely old guy. His dog panted and whined beside him but the moment he glared at it the mutt lay silent.

You get tired of haulin your boards out from town, you can leave em at our place.

Neither Loonie nor I said anything to this; we didn't know how to respond.

I'm away a bit, said the bloke. But you can shove em under the house. The missus won't mind.

Geez, I said. Thanks.

No worries.

First driveway. Just up here.

Okay.

He drove off and we looked at one another with a dumb shrug. I wasn't ready to leave my precious board at anyone's place but my own, yet I was flushed warm from the attention. On our way back, weaving up the bitumen one-handed, with our boards yawing and straining under our arms, we pedalled by the turnoff we'd never paid any mind to before. It was marked with an old green-painted fridge and the dirt track in was rutted and steep. From the road there was no sign of a house, only a wall of karri trees on the ridge. The land was fenced but this wasn't any sort of farm.

Hippies, said Loonie.

We coasted down to the swampy flats and caught our breaths for the hard uphill plug into town.

I never suspected I'd be sent to school thirty miles away in Angelus, and I'm not even sure why my parents enrolled me there. At the time they said it was to give me stability, a high school where I could go right through to my senior year, but I had an inkling it was a manoeuvre to limit Loonie's influence. They waited until after New Year's to spring the news, and I was so stunned that I didn't even put up a fight. I was just glad they hadn't sent me to board at the hostel, though I'm certain they'd have been unable to endure the separation. Still, such tenderness condemned me to years of bussing, and the bus ride is my chief memory of high school – the smells of vinyl and diesel and toothpaste, corrugated-iron shelters out by the highway, rain-soaked farmkids, the funk of wet wool and greasy scalps, the staccato rattle of the perspex emergency window, the silent feuds and the low-gear labouring behind pig trucks, the spidery handwriting of homework done in your lap, and the heartbreaking winter dusk that greeted you as the bus rolled back across the bridge into Sawyer.

The bus dropped me into a kind of limbo. Until I'd hooked up with Loonie I'd been a loner, and now that I finally had a mate I'd been turned into a dayboy. I could never expect to belong in a big town like Angelus – I was a total stranger there – but now I wouldn't even fit properly into my hometown. Everyone knew proper locals went to the Ag School, while kids who caught the bus to Angelus, dags like me and the banker's daughter, were of some indeterminate species. We were so uncertain of our new status, we never spoke to one another from one term to the next.

Angelus with its harbour and shops and railhead was a regional hub. The department store and silos and ships gave it gravity but I refused to be impressed. Even so, with the passage of time a kind of contempt for Sawyer crept up on me as I saw how tiny and static and insignificant it really was. Like my parents, it was so drab and fixed that it became embarrassing. During the school holidays, in the years before every failing dairy farm was bought up and turned into a winery or a yuppie bed-and-breakfast, people drove down from the city in their Triumphs and Mercs to look at our little timber houses and shop verandahs and the shambolic superstructure of the mill. They trickled in from their romantic drives through the karri forests and the remnant stands of giant tingle to fuel up and amuse themselves at the pub and bakery. Every time I heard the word *quaint* I was caught between shame and fury.

During school term I only saw Loonie on weekends. When conditions were good we rode out to the coast to surf but the ride seemed to get longer and harder the more we did it and in the end we gave up humping our boards all the way and took up the offer to stash them at the house close by. That was how we got to know Sando, how our lives took such a turn.

We didn't actually see the big, woolly-headed bloke much the first summer that I was in high school. Whenever a big sou'west swell kicked up, we looked for him. Those were the days when the Angelus crew came out in their panel vans and utes. They were tradies and potheads who kept an eye on the weather map and took sickies every time there was surf, but the most we saw of the bloke with the flat-tray Volkswagen were the times we caught a glimpse of him far down the bay, just a silhouette paddling a surfski and trolling for early salmon.

The first time we stumped up the drive to his house the place was deserted. No dog came barrelling out of the shadows and no one emerged when we called from the bottom of the steps. We stood in the leaf-littered clearing and just stared at the joint. There was a big, fenced vegetable garden and some odd-looking outbuildings and though the house was built from local timber it was like no home I'd ever seen. It stood high off the ground on log-poles, surrounded by spacious verandahs where hammocks and mobiles and shell-chains hung twisting in the breeze. None of the wood was painted and all those timbers had gone their own shades of weathered grey and khaki. Later I thought of the house as a kind of elevated safari tent, a tent whose every pole was an old-growth log that three men could barely link arms around.

Jesus, said Loonie.

We better go, I murmured, but Loonie was already halfway up the front stairs.

Bloody hell, he said from up there. Carn, Pikelet, check it out.

I hesitated until he started gobbing over the rail. I went up full of misgivings. From the verandah you could see the ocean and the eastern cliffs toward Angelus. Closer in, the estuary was like a wide, shining gut that was fed by the river as it coiled back and back on itself into the blue-green blur of the forest beyond the town. I'd never thought of the river as an intestine but then I'd never viewed the country from this angle before and seen just how shaggy and animal its contours were. The house sat behind a snarl of karri regrowth that hid it from the coast road a couple of hundred yards below. The property had some lumpy pasture on its eastern side, a steep and hopeless paddock that looked as if it fed only roos and rabbits. The rest of it was peppermint thicket and wattles that ran right up to the forest ridges.

Behind the French doors, the interior of the house

seemed to be mostly one enormous room with rugs on the floor, a stone fireplace and a table as big as a lifeboat. Above this, set against the far gable, was a broad, open sleeping loft. There were no blinds or curtains anywhere, only a few sarongs that hung like flags from beams. Not even Loonie had the nerve to check if the doors were locked, but it looked as if the place had been empty for weeks. We gazed out again at the watertank, at the wood-slab sheds and our bikes and boards propped in the dappled light beneath the solitary marri tree. We looked for somewhere to store our boards.

Beneath the house was a kind of wood-louvred undercroft stacked with surfboards and wave-skis and a kayak. The ground was leafy underfoot and there was a cave smell about everything. Further in stood a weights bench and dumbbells, a stool or two and a long worktable neatly piled with tools and papers and sound cassettes.

Far out, said Loonie. This is bloody paradise.

We stood openmouthed before the racks of boards. There was every type and shape and vintage, some with fins like scythes and others with twin keels. One board, which had to be twelve feet long, was made of solid wood. Beside it, propped against the wall and made of something like the same stuff, was a didjeridu with such a twist in the shaft it looked like a hollow tree root.

Don't touch anything, I said, expecting someone to

arrive at any moment. Let's just get our boards and stick em somewhere and rack off.

Don't be so uptight, Pikelet. The bloke said it was okay.

To leave our boards here, I said. Not to hang around.

Loonie laughed at my anxious propriety, but he helped me stow our boards beneath the worktable and a few minutes later we were bouncing down the track half afraid and half hoping the VW would come wallowing up to intercept us. But nobody came. We rode back into Sawyer with a glow on, as though by simply having stashed our boards beneath such a house, we'd moved up in the world.

HONKING AWAY on my old didj, I think about the one I first saw nestled against the boards under that big hippy house. I hardly knew what it was. Now the wind comes through me in circles, like a memory, one breath, without pause, hot and long. It's funny, but you never really think much about breathing. Until it's all you ever think about. I consider the startled look on the faces of my girls in the moments after each of them was born and suctioned and forced to draw air in for the first time. I've done the job myself on more than one occasion, pulled over on the side of an ill-lit street, improvising in someone's driveway. Always the same puzzled look, the rude shock of respiration, as though the child's drawn in a gutful of fire. Yet within a moment or two the whole procedure is normalized, automatic. In a whole lifetime you might rarely give it another thought. Until you have your first asthma attack or come upon some stranger trying to drag air into himself with such effort that the stuff could be as thick and heavy as honey. Or you may be like me and think about breathing often enough for people to have their doubts about you.

I've been thinking about the enigma of respiration as long as I can remember, since I was old enough to be aware of the old man coming home with his stink of grease and sweat and wood-sap at the end of another day at the mill. Every weekday evening after he washed his face and hands he'd settle at the table and look about with eyes bloodshot from sawdust while Mum whacked the handle of the oven with a length of split karri and drew out whatever she'd been baking or roasting or warming while we waited for him. Mostly we ate in silence. Afterwards I'd go to my room to do my homework and when I came back later to watch a bit of TV, the old man'd still be there, asleep in his chair, with the wireless on softly. Mum and I would wash the dishes before she helped him to bed, and I'd sit down for an hour in front of the box.

Long before I even turned in I'd hear him begin to snore, but it was later, in the quiet of the night, when he really got going. I don't know how my mother endured it, how she ever slept at all, for there were nights when I lay completely and hopelessly awake while he sawed away at the other end of the house. The noise wasn't the worst of it. It was the pauses that really got to me. When he fell silent I'd lie there waiting, forced to listen to my own breathing which was so steady and involuntary. More than once since then I've wondered whether the life-threatening high jinks that Loonie and I and Sando and Eva got up to in the years of my adolescence were anything more than a rebellion against the monotony of drawing breath. It's easy for an old man to look back and see the obvious, how wasted youth and health and safety are on the young who spurn such things, to be dismayed by the risks you took, but as a youth you do sense that life renders you powerless by dragging you back to it, breath upon breath upon breath in an endless capitulation to biological routine, and that the human will to control is as much about asserting power over your own body as exercising it on others.

Loonie and I acted out the impulse without thinking, for dumb larks. We held our breaths and counted. We timed ourselves in the river and the ocean, in the old man's shed or in the broken autumn light of the forest floor. It takes quite some concentration and willpower to defy the logic of your own body, to take yourself to the shimmering edge. It seems bizarre, looking back, to realize just how hard we worked at this. We were good at it and in our own minds it's what set us apart from everyone else.

Deep diving and breath-holding against the clock seemed a more impressive endeavour than the game played by boys at the Ag School. Loonie told me how one kid would spend a minute or so hyperventilating until he was dizzy and when he was seeing spots a mate would hug him from behind so hard and so suddenly that all the air was crushed from his chest. Often as not, the kid simply blacked out and fell to the ground. Some puked and one even had convulsions, though Loonie suspected faking. Loonie and I tried it a few times. When he flat-out fainted I went into a panic. He came to with a strange moan and a stupid look on his face. Then he did it to me and I went down with a curious tunnel vision and the whole frame of my consciousness seemed to melt at the edges before giving way entirely. Afterwards I puked a little and laughed but I felt like an Ag School idiot and wasn't keen to repeat the experience. The attraction was plain enough – it was cheap weirdness in the days before we knew about drugs – but only later did I understand the physiology of it.

It was some years before I realized that when the old man paused mid-snore on those nights back in Sawyer and I lay there for long seconds in a mixture of relief and anticipation, he'd done more than simply stop snoring. He'd actually stopped breathing. At the end of those silences he'd let out a kind of braying gasp, like a man who'd just seen a ghost – perhaps the ghost of himself – and this was the sound of his body yanking him back to the surface from the limbo of apnoea, hauling him back to life itself. Mum must have heard dead-halts like this night after night for decades. How did she bear it, lying beside him, abandoned, listening for his return?

NEXT TIME we went to the log house, the VW was there in the shade of the marri tree and the red kelpie shot out from beneath the stairs. I was fending the mutt off when a woman came out onto the verandah above us.

You boys take a wrong turn?

Just came to get our boards, said Loonie.

Duke! she yelled at the dog. Get down, goddammit.

The dog took one last lick and desisted, and the woman, who looked to be in her twenties, squinted doubtfully at us. She had ropy white plaits and an American accent.

They're under the house, I said.

Are they, now?

Red and green, I said. A Jacko and a Hawke.

Bloke said we could, said Loonie.

She sighed and stared at us another moment before coming barefoot down the stairs. She held the handrail as though she might fall. She wore jeans and a tee-shirt that said *freestylin: watch me fly*.

You better show me, she said with a tone of weary scepticism.

We followed her into the cave-like undercroft to point out our modest craft beneath the bench, and as we drew them out their dings and welts and browning contusions seemed magnified. They were sorry bits of junk but they were clearly ours.

He's not here, she said.

Oh? said Loonie in the bright tone he reserved for indulging adults when the mood suited. See, we saw the Vee-dub and thought, well, that he was around.

No. He's away.

Angelus? I asked with the board under my arm, my body already turned for the doorway.

The islands.

What islands? said Loonie.

Indonesia.

The woman spoke the word as if it had extra syllables. Indonesia. Neither of us even knew with any certainty where Indonesia was.

Well, I said. Thanks.

Sure, she said without warmth.

Orright if we drop em back later? asked Loonie. Cause, we didn't ask. Your bloke, he offered.

The woman gave a wan smile and limped out into the light. Her feet were brown and the frayed hems of her Levi's hung back off her heels. She didn't answer. She simply waved us away and pulled herself back up the stairs. We bolted while we had the chance.

The surf at the Point that day was bigger than either of us expected. The steadily rising swell seemed to match the oily cloud pouring in from the south, and the longer we stayed, the bigger and gloomier it got out there on the water. We sat in the line-up with a few of the Angelus crew, who let us have a smaller wave now and then, but by afternoon we were paddling much more than surfing and the pack was moving further and further seaward to meet the hulking sets. Despite the building swell, the older blokes kept up their constant sledging and bantering, but Loonie and I were silent. My skin seemed to tighten on me. I felt the new mood in the group, tried to read something in every sideways glance and raised eyebrow, and each time somebody began to casually stroke seaward I followed for safety's sake, and found that I was not alone; we all moved out together. It was as though we became one strange beast, like a school of fish moving wordlessly in unison. There was always a moment when a fresh conviction came into our stroke. We put our heads down and paddled for all we were worth, even though more than half of us hadn't yet seen the chains of swell beginning to warp into the bay. Eventually we'd see the set trundling in, looking for all the world as if the whole rolling column might simply grind past the Point toward the misty smudges of the eastern cliffs in the distance, but then the shoaling underwater ridge of the headland snagged those waves one by one, swinging them in like gates hinged upon the land itself until they turned shoreward in our direction.

This wasn't Sawyer Point anymore. This was outside – Outside Sawyer Point, as the older guys called it – and it hadn't broken like this for a year.

I was galvanized by fear. I had no intention of surfing these waves – they were way out of my range – but neither did I want to be mown down by them, so I paddled like hell to scrape up and over each in turn before they broke. I felt Loonie nearby doing more or less the same thing, though a tad more coolly, and I remember making it up the spray-torn crest of an absolute smoker just as some goateed hellman dropped blithely down its face. In that instant I turned to see that the tip of the headland was, as I suspected, behind us. We were now beyond the Point, outside the bay. It was only five hundred yards but it truly felt like we were at sea.

Other more experienced riders caught waves around us. They flew past hooting and screaming until in an eerie lull after a long passage of swells I realized that there were only three of us left out there – Loonie and me and a bloke from Angelus called Slipper. Slipper had a matted ginger Afro and the bloodshot eyes of a stoner. Two of his front teeth were missing and he wore an old beavertail dive suit that looked like a dingo had been at it. He sat up beside us and smiled as if he was having the time of his life. I, it must be said, was not nearly as sanguine.

Take the next one, kid, he said.

Aw, I dunno, I murmured.

Can't walk home from here, he said with a manic leer. May's well go for it, eh? How bout you, Snowy? You goin? No point bobbin around out here like a bloody teabag.

Orright, said Loonie rising to the bait. I'll go.

The rip that poured seaward from the bay had become a veritable river surging past the rocks of the headland to spew a plume of sand and weed at our backs. We found ourselves forced further and further out by the current. The sea became confused and jumpy. We were in foreign territory now. The coast to the west was a snarl of cliffs and boulders into the murky distance; there was nowhere to land over there. I considered paddling back east across the rip and into the bay to aim for the bar at the rivermouth, but that would put me right in the path of the oncoming sets and I'd be buried in whitewater. I knew that once I lost my board I'd be at the mercy of the current and I didn't like my chances. There was no way around the fact that I was buggered. I was so frightened I genuinely thought I could shit myself at any moment.

Slipper called a heads-up as another set began to bear down on us. It was much further seaward of where we were but it looked ready to break even that far out. In such a depth of water the very idea of this was stupefying.

You're not gunna pike on me, are youse? Slipper bellowed over his shoulder. You won't choke now, willya Snow?

Piss off, said Loonie with a sick grin.

Just remember, I'm givin youse a wave. Don't usually hand out freebies to little snot-nose grommets, but I'm in a good mood, so take it while it's goin.

The first wave of that set was lumpy and malformed but Loonie turned and went anyway as I knew he would. The soles of his feet looked yellow and small, and his elbows stuck out as he paddled. I sat, rearing a moment, as all that water welled up beneath us. And then he was gone.

Slipper hooted. But in a moment another wedging peak was upon us.

Carn, kid. No guts no glory.

I don't think so, I said.

It's the only way home now.

I said nothing.

Ya mate'll know you're a sook, a fuckin pussy.

But I didn't go. I just barely made it up the face of that wave and freefell out the back so hard I had the wind knocked out of me. Slipper paddled up close and snarled in my ear.

I take the next one, sport, and you're out here on yer own. Get it?

By then I was addled and breathless. Loonie's wave was spilling itself across the rivermouth already but there was no sign of him.

The third wave began its slow left turn towards me. It looked as big as the pub and as it began to break the sound rattled my ribs. With Slipper right up beside me I turned my little stubby Hawke around and paddled. I paddled, I must add, without vigour, and in a moment the wave was upon me, its mass overtaking me so fast that it felt as though I was travelling backwards. All about was seething vapour. I hung right up in the boiling nest of foam at its very peak, suspended in noise and unbelief, before I began to fall out and down in a welter of blinding spray. I only got to my feet from instinct, but there I suddenly was, upright and alive, skittering in front of all that jawing mess with my little board chattering underfoot. It was hard to credit the speed, the way the wave hauled itself upright in my path as it found shallower water. All I could do was squat and aim in hope. Yet for all this mad acceleration there was still something ponderous about the movement of the water. On TV I'd seen elephants run beside safari jeeps, pounding along at incredible speed while seeming to move in slow motion, and that's exactly how it was: hectic noise, immense force driven up through the feet and knees, all in a kind of stoptime.

For a fatal moment, now that I was unexpectedly on top of things, the whole enterprise seemed too easy. Within three seconds I went from saving myself from certain disaster to believing I was a thirteen-year-old hellman.

I never did see the great slab of water that cut me off at the knees. Loonie said it came down behind like a landslip and simply flicked me away. I didn't even get time to draw a breath. I was abruptly in darkness, being poleaxed across the sandy bottom of the bay, holding onto the dregs in my lungs while the grit blasted through my hair and my limbs felt as though they would be wrenched from their sockets. When I burst back to the surface my board was long gone, and before I could begin the swim in another rumbling pile of foam bore down on me so I dived and took another belting. It seemed a good while before I finally came up in a spritzing froth in the shallows, sinuses burning, shorts around my thighs, and by then Loonie was already up on the beach, grinning like a nutter, with my board stuck tail-first into the dry sand beside him.

Slipper came in on the wave of the day. He wound his way across the bay in long, arrogant swipes, flicked out in front of the rivermouth and walked all the way back up the beach as nonchalant as you like. But as he reached us he gave a gap-toothed leer, tossed his board onto the flatbed truck and motioned for us to throw ours on as well. We didn't hesitate. We climbed up beside the Angelus crew, basking in their new and grudging respect, and as we ground up the track a monster set closed out the entire bay behind us, shooting foam against the dunes and brown stormscum high across the scrub of the headland. It was carnage. And yet the swell still appeared to be building.

The truck reached the dirt turnaround where our bikes lay, but it didn't stop. We veered west into a set of wheel ruts that traversed the ridge of the headland and crossed into heath country – spiky, wild scrub dotted with granite boulders and washouts. Boards and tools and bodies slammed back and forth across the tray until we pulled up a mile or so further on at a basalt knoll above the sea cliffs.

Everyone stood and leant on the roof of the cab, staring seaward. I didn't know what we were all looking at. And then I saw the flickering white bombora in the distance.

When the bay shuts down, said Slipper, it starts to crank out there.

A mile out, a white smear appeared on the black sea. A moment later the sound of it reached us. It was like a thunderclap; you could feel the vibration in the chassis of the truck.

How big is that? I asked.

Everybody laughed.

Well, I persisted, how big was the Point today?

Too big for *you*, sport, said Slipper.

Eight foot, maybe, said someone. Ten right there at the end.

So what's that? I persisted. Out there. What size?

Slipper shrugged. Can't tell, he said. Twenty?

Bigger, said a wiry little bloke.

Does anyone surf it?

Nobody spoke.

Fuck that, said Slipper at last. It's sharky as shit out there.

The sea was dark now and the sky even blacker. Vapour hung in shrouds above the cliffs. Quite suddenly and with great force it began to rain. We jounced back towards the Point in the downpour and I looked at Loonie and saw that no amount of rain could spoil the day for him. His lip was split from grinning. He'd ridden his wave all the way to the beach. There was a glory about him. He was untouchable.

From the shelter of her big verandah the American woman looked down at the pair of us. We stood sodden and shivering in the mud of her yard.

I guess you better come up, she said.

We stashed our boards under the house and slopped upstairs to find that she had some old towels out for us and when we were more or less dry she let us in through the French doors.

Inside the place smelled of incense. A fire snapped in the hearth and there was music playing.

Coffee?

We nodded and she told us to stand by the fire.

It sounds big down there, she said without enthusiasm.

Ten foot, said Loonie.

Huh. Too big for you guys.

We handled it, said Loonie.

Oh, sure you did.

We got witnesses.

She half smiled and poured us mugs of coffee from a glass jug. Through the windows you could see the storm descending on the coast. Sawyer and the forest were obscured by rain.

You're from America? I asked.

California, she said. Before that, Utah, I guess.

Calafawnya, said Loonie in crude imitation. Yoo-tar. So how come you're *here*?

Hey, I ask myself. Drink up and I'll drive you back to town.

We're orright, said Loonie.

Sure. But I'm going in anyways. I guess you're from Sawyer, huh?

Neither of us said anything to this and I thought about how obviously local we must have looked in our flannel shirts and Blundstones. I took my cue from Loonie and slugged back the coffee as best I could. No amount of sugar could make up for the oily bitterness of it. We Pikes were strictly tea drinkers; this was the first coffee I'd ever drunk.

We drove into town without speaking. The Volkswagen shuddered with every gust; its wipers were helpless against the deluge. It felt weird being pressed close in that narrow cab with a woman.

At the end of my drive we both got out but Loonie leaned back in the open door.

It was ten foot today, he said. And we rode it. Can you tell him?

Sure, she said. The moment he arrives.

What's your name? he said with mortifying familiarity.

Eva.

Thanks for the lift, then. Eva.

She revved up the old eggbeater and I pulled our bikes down while he stood there grinning.

Close the door, kid.

But Loonie kept standing there in the rain while the engine sputtered and gulped. His smile was a provocation. The Volkswagen jerked forward. The door slammed shut. We watched her drive on through the downpour.

She likes me, said Loonie.

Yeah, right.

Hey, maybe your Mum's done scones.

We pedalled hard for the house.

THERE WAS ALWAYS a manic energy about Loonie, some strange hotwired spirit that made you laugh with shock. He hurled himself at the world. You could never second-guess him and once he embarked upon something there was no holding him back. Yet the same stuff you marvelled at could really wear you down. Some Mondays I was relieved to be back on the bus to school.

Nothing would have made me own up to this at the time but I actually liked being in school. There was a soothing dullness in the classroom, a calm in which part of me thrived. Could be it was the orderly home I grew up in, the safety of always knowing what came next. In any case my experience of school was not at all like

Loonie's. For me there was no constant locking of horns, no dangerous visibility. I liked books – the respite and privacy of them – books about plants and the formation of ice and the business of world wars. Whenever I sank into them I felt free. If Loonie wasn't around I tended to go unnoticed and I suppose that in earlier years this had made me lonely, but now a bit of solitude was welcome.

After school sometimes, if there was light enough, I walked up into the state forest to wander about alone. I knew that somewhere in there, near an old sawpit, the Ag School boys had hell's own flying fox. Loonie boasted of shots across the river through the swaying crowns of trees. He talked up the roar of the cable, the sensation of your arms almost coming out of their sockets. He was forever at me to go out with him before the rangers finally found where it was and cut it down, but I was leery of the Ag School crowd and in truth I preferred to be out in the forest alone.

Whenever I went up through that timber country I made sure to keep the fact from my parents. It was another deception that became routine, for they were like all the other old folks in town in that the forest made them as uneasy as the sea. Locals might venture out in gangs for felling, but no one seemed to like to go alone, and certainly not without a practical reason to be there. Nobody ever said they were scared, but that's all it was and I could understand it, for there was stuff out there that creaked and thwacked and groaned. Any kind of breeze up in those karris and tingles made a roar that set the hair up on the back of your neck. You walked around in that crowded landscape and some part of your brain refused to accept the fact you were alone. I liked to wind my way up the ridges until Sawyer was obscured by trees and not even the distant sea was visible. Then I'd plunge over into the back-country where only the morning sun penetrated and I never saw a soul. I came home at dusk with my ears ringing from the quiet.

WE RODE OUT to the coast one sunny morning in spring and climbed the drive at the hippy house to get our boards and saw that Sando was back. In those days we still didn't even know his name. He looked up from the board he was buffing across two sawhorses. He was bareback in the mild sun. He let the machine hang by its cord at his side. His dog charged across the clearing towards us.

Well, he said. If it isn't Heckle and Jeckle.

Eva limped out onto the verandah long enough to see who it was before going back in again.

You timed it perfect for a lift, he said running a hand

across the glossy gel-coat of the new board. Just going down to try this out.

He turned the board over. It was small and disc-shaped with twin keels. He'd tinted it banana yellow.

Wax this up for me, willya? Be back in a minute.

Loonie and I found blocks of wax beneath the house. We returned to the sawhorses and stood each side of the spanking-new board, speechless with wonder. All we could do was run our hands down its shiny-smooth rails. It seemed improper to soil such a beautiful thing with wax and when Sando came back downstairs with his wetsuit we were still standing there awestruck.

There was only a small swell running that day and nobody was out at the Point except us. We took waves in turns. The water was clear and the rip was mild. Sando skated around on his little yellow disc, pushing it about, experimenting in the waist-high waves. There was a casual authority in the way he surfed, a grace that made all our moves look jerky and hesitant. He was a big, strong man. The tight wetsuit showed every contour of his body, the width of his shoulders, the meat in his thighs. Water shone in his beard. His eyes were steely in the glare. In the long lulls we bobbed either side of him, our feet pedalling idly. We were bashful in his presence.

The missus says you blokes had a bit of a swell while I was gone.

Loonie filled him in about the storm and those waves cranking in from outside the headland. He talked about the Angelus crew and our epic rides across the bay. Once he got going there was no turning him; everything in his telling got bigger and gnarlier – our courage was unfathomable, our style in the face of danger something to behold. Sando laughed indulgently, sceptical. He said Loonie talked a good game and this only drove Loonie on to telling him that we'd driven out along the ridges and cliffs to see the bombora breaking.

Ah, said Sando. Old Smoky. That's what it's called.

Has anyone surfed it? I asked.

Sando studied me a moment. Well, he murmured. That'd be telling, wouldn't it.

It must have been twenty feet, said Loonie.

It's a big, wild coast out that way, said Sando. All kinds of surprises out there. Fun and games, for the discreet gentleman.

He had an odd, dreamy way of speaking and we sat alongside him mesmerized until a small wave popped into view and Sando whipped around and dropped in without even paddling. I watched the yellow blur of his board through the glassy back of the wave. I saw the flash of his hands, his arms cast up. He was dancing.

LOONIE AND I were out at Sando's a lot that spring. We came and went with our boards, hoping he was home or down at the Point, but often as not his place was deserted. If he was around and in the mood, he showed us how to read weather maps and predict swell conditions, or he'd teach us to use fibreglass and resin to repair the dings in our boards. Yet there were days out at the Point when he wouldn't even acknowledge our presence, especially if the Angelus crew was over. He sat out beyond everybody, waiting for the intermittent sneaker, the wave of the hour, and when he caught one he came flying by the rest of us, his big, prehensile feet spread across the deck like something strange and immoveable. On those days his eyes were glassy and distant, with not a flicker of recognition.

Some afternoons in the shade beneath his house he told quiet stories of the islands: treks through paddies and palm groves to cliff villages and caves; the smells of incense and drying fish and coconut oil; reefs that villagers paddled him out to in outrigger canoes, and waves that wound perfectly across acres of coral.

Sando made some boards for himself, planing them into shape out there in the yard, though now and then new boards were delivered to him wrapped in the cardboard of old fridge boxes and bound with gaffer tape. He wouldn't tell us what the deal was or who sent them, and on more than one occasion I slipped behind the shed where he stacked the packaging before he shredded it all for compost, and furtively scanned the senders' addresses in Perth, Sydney, San Francisco and Maui. There was one from Peru, another from Mauritius. Boards came and boards went. He rode some and others simply disappeared.

In November we began to cut weeds for him and plugged holes in his drive with buckets of gravel. Sometimes he paid us, but mostly we were glad of the chance to be around him. Sando was quite unlike other men we knew. There were a couple teachers I didn't mind, but you could never forget the fact that they were being paid to seem interested in you. Sando wasn't nearly so eager. He simply consented, when it suited him, to have us about the place. He was often aloof and he could be fickle. At times there was a palpable restraint in his manner, a sense that he could say a good deal more than he did.

Those rare times we were invited into the house proper, I noted the masks and carvings on the walls, the woven hangings and bone artefacts from places I could only guess at. The wall opposite the fireplace was loaded with books: Jack London, Conrad, Melville, Hans Hass, Cousteau, Lao Tzu, Carlos Castaneda. Abalone shells lay polished on a coffee table, and there were brass oil lamps, his didjeridu and the vertebra of a right whale like a big, pockmarked stool.

In those early days, whenever Eva was around, Sando was formal with us, even a little circumspect. Eva was often tired and only seemed to tolerate our presence for his sake. The few times I considered her for more than a moment she struck me as a brooder, an unhappy soul. I caught the faces she made at callow things we said; she could give the most neutral turn of phrase a sarcastic edge, so I did my best to avoid her. All my attention was on Sando anyway. I loved being around that huge, bearded, coiled-up presence. His body was a map of where he'd been. He had great bumps on his knees and feet from old-school surfing, his forearms were pulpy with reef-scars and years of sun had bleached his hair and beard. He was, for us, a delicious enigma. He never quite did what we might expect him to do and there wasn't a man in Sawyer or Angelus in his league.

During the last good swell of the season, on a Saturday at the Point when the Angelus crew was over and Loonie and I were out trading waves with them at the very end of the headland, taking drops so steep that our guts rose to the back of our throats, Sando turned up on the beach without a board, pulled on a pair of fins and swam out in his Speedos to bodysurf the biggest sets of the day. He never even nodded in our direction. Between waves he bobbed in the rip like a seal, as though he didn't share our DNA, let alone our language. Ten of us sat there in the noise and spray doing our best not to stare at him, because even without a board he outsurfed us all. Nobody dared paddle for a wave that Sando showed interest in. For the first time as surfers we found ourselves – man and boy – deferring to a mere swimmer. When he shot in to the beach one last time and flicked off his fins and walked up into the trees, I think most of us were disappointed to see him go.

I WAS PEDALLING alone on the coast road one day in December when I saw Sando's VW pulled up askew on the gravel shoulder. Dark smudges of rubber stretched back along the bitumen and when I arrived he was standing over a crippled roo. I saw the jack handle at his side. He looked miserable and angry. The intensity of his gaze scared me.

This is what you get, he said. This is what happens. And isn't it lovely.

He killed the animal with a couple of blows to the head, then hoisted it onto the tray of the Volkswagen and looked back up the road to where it must have leapt out. It was a western grey and not a big one. I wondered what he was doing with it. Other people just dragged a carcass off the road and out of the way; some didn't even go to that much trouble. On the varnished pine flatbed, the roo's blood was impossibly bright.

Well, said Sando. Come if you're comin.

I threw my bike up beside the roadkill and climbed in beside him. He smelled of sweat and animal. He didn't speak and I didn't dare ask questions. When we got to his place he got out and tied up the dog. He went into a shed and came back with a meat hook and a length of rope. I stood by while he strung the roo up by the tail. Then he stalked off to the house and left me there beneath the marri tree. From up at the house there was muffled shouting. Eva sounded upset but I couldn't hear what she said. The dog whined, tugged at its chain.

The roo twisted on the rope and blood dripped slower and slower from its snout to the leaf litter below. With its forepaws outstretched, the animal looked as though it was caught in a perpetual earthward dive. I stared at it a long time. The roo aimed and aimed and never arrived. Only its blood made the journey. I thought of it at the roadside, in the heavy thicket, gathering itself to leap across the bitumen. I wondered if kangaroos had thoughts. Because if they did, then it seemed to me that this roo's intentions might have made it across the road, landing ahead of it the way its blood did even now. The idea made me a bit giddy. I'd never thought something like this before.

Sando came back with a knife and steel. He was agitated, but honing the blade seemed to calm him.

It's the least we can do, he said. Waste of life, waste of protein.

Yeah, I said uncertainly.

Lean meat, he said.

I didn't reply. I watched him skin the carcass and then open it up so that its entrails poured out onto the ground.

I gotta go, I said.

Wait, he said. Take some home to your oldies.

I stood there grimly, shrinking from him a little. He seemed to know how to butcher a beast but it was obvious that he was from the city. Otherwise he'd have known that my oldies wouldn't eat roo meat in a million years. We didn't even have a dog we could feed it to. Kangaroo was like rabbit; it was what you ate when you were poor and hopeless, and you sure as hell didn't eat roadkill of any description.

Eventually Sando sent me on my way with two cord-like fillets in a flourbag that I hoiked into the bushes on the ride back to Sawyer.

SUMMER CAME and the holidays with it, but the sea was mostly flat. One surfless afternoon Loonie and I pushed our bikes up Sando's drive in search of something to do, but he and Eva were out. The sheds were locked and the car gone. Only the dog was there. We waited around in the hope that Sando would show up but it was clear that we'd made the long ride for nothing.

For a while we sat on the steps pinging bits of gravel at the tree where the hook and rope still hung. I didn't tell Loonie about the roo business; I didn't know how to represent the peculiarity of it to him without making Sando seem ridiculous. Loonie was a harsh judge of people and talking about the roo would have made me feel disloyal. Besides, I'd gone riding alone that day in the hope of finding Sando and having him to myself for a bit, and I didn't want Loonie to know. After we got bored throwing rocks we started prowling about in the cool shade beneath the house, looking at all the boards hanging in their racks, and it was there that we found the banana box full of surf magazines that somebody had left on top of our own boards beneath the work-bench. I was annoyed to find a box dumped on our gear. I yanked it out and dropped it on the benchtop. Loonie snatched a magazine off the stack and flicked through. It was an old number from the sixties with black and white photos that featured riders with short hair and boards like planks. I rifled through the box and found others of more recent vintage that were printed in colour.

They were American magazines, lavish and confident in their production, with a welter of ads and products and images of famous riders at Hawaiian breaks like Sunset Beach and Pipeline and Makaha. Within a few minutes I began to recognize a familiar stance, a silhouette I knew very well.

Shit, I said. Look!

Loonie leant over and didn't really need to follow the caption beneath my finger.

Billy Sanderson, styling at Rocky Point. Jesus!

Look. There's more.

We strewed the contents of the box across the bench and clawed through them to find other images of Sando. There he was, in Maui in 1970, in Morocco in the winter of '68, and at the Hollister Ranch in '71. I found him in aviator shades and a Billy Jack hat in a full-page ad for Dewey Weber boards. There was even an old picture of him as a jug-eared kid in sandshoes, noseriding a longboard with his back arched and his arm and head thrown back like a matador: *The urchin and the urchins – Australia's Bill Sanderson, Spiny Reef.*

For an hour and more Loonie and I tried to piece together a story from all these disparate captions and photos, but all we could really glean was the fact that Sando – for a time, and in places that were legendary to the likes of us – had briefly *been somebody.* I felt stupid for not having known, and somehow the shame of this, and the realization that Sando had kept it from us, dampened the excitement of the discovery.

Then the dog mysteriously deserted us and a moment later the VW lurched up into the clearing. We hurled everything back into the cardboard box but before we had it stowed beneath the bench Sando was in the doorway. The smile slipped sideways from his face.

Loonie and I spent half an hour sitting on the bottom step while Eva and Sando bickered and squalled up in the house. We looked dolefully at our bikes, longing to escape this scene, but neither of us had the nerve to defy Sando whose request for us to stay and wait was delivered with the gravity of an order.

What game are you playing? he yelled at her. What was the fucking point of that?

Well, you're their guru, aren't you? Eva screamed. Don't they get to touch your holy relics, read your scriptures? Deep down, didn't you secretly want me to *reveal* you to your disciples?

You know what I think about that shit. I don't understand you.

Well, right on, Billy. You finally got there on your own; you don't understand me at all.

Don't be bitter.

You don't have the goddamn right to tell me not to be bitter.

You're only like this —

Like what, honey? Nasty? Don't you like nasty no more?

Jealous isn't just nasty, Eva. It's sad.

Then she was crying. A tap began to run and when it stopped the pipes clanked. In the fresh quiet, the dog came back downstairs to sniff at us and spread its rank meat-breath around. I couldn't help but think of the roo.

Shit, said Loonie. They're gunna kiss'n make up. Let's go.

No, I murmured. Wait.

I thought of the look on Sando's face, how instantly he'd read us. Before he'd even seen the mags he'd sensed something different in the way we looked at him. It was hard to believe that we'd been so obvious. But it was true. Our admiration for him had enlarged; it had metastasized. I remembered how we leapt out of his way as he lunged for the box. He stood back with it under his arm like a man holding something dangerous and unstable and I had the queerest feeling of having transgressed. His gaze was more wounded than fierce, not unlike the queasy misunderstood look old soldiers gave you from the pub verandah.

But when he came back downstairs he'd lost that look. He just seemed exhausted and stood there a moment while the dog licked his big bony feet.

Didn't mean to piss anyone off, said Loonie.

Oh, it's just old crap, he murmured. Forget it. Load up and I'll drive you back into town.

For a good mile on the way home there was no talk. The cab always felt pretty snug but now it seemed way too small for the three of us. I was conscious of Sando's clean animal scent and the size of his fist on the gearstick.

Listen, he said at last. Eva's doin it tough, just now. It's a hard time for her.

Neither Loonie nor I knew quite what to say to this.

And I've been away a lot. So.

We puttered along the edge of the estuary where the sloughing white skins of melaleucas spilled onto the road.

Is it the pills? asked Loonie.

I glared at him in surprise. I'd never seen any pills.

She takes pills, said Loonie defiantly. I seen her.

There was a long pause.

No, said Sando. It's not really the pills.

I sat there in a funk. Loonie hadn't even told me.

She's always bloody cranky, said Loonie. I just figured it was them, that's all.

Just shut up, I hissed. It's none of our business.

And it's not what you think, anyway, said Sando.

Loonie shrugged. The gesture was defiant, so emphatic in that tight space it hoisted my shirt an inch. He was sullen the rest of the way back and when it became clear that he was being dropped off first, his mood darkened further. Outside the pub he got down, pulled his bike off the tray and wheeled it away without a word.

The mags, I said to Sando. They were just there. On our boards.

All in the past, mate. No worries.

How badly I wanted to say something about the photos then, just a gesture of esteem, but it was clear this wouldn't be welcome. There was something about Sando that wasn't settled. He wasn't fixed like my father, and intrigued as I was I found this aspect of him confusing to the point of anxiety. It was as though he wasn't quite as old as he looked, as if he hadn't yet finished with himself.

Tell Loonie not to be too uptight about the pills, he said. They're just painkillers.

We can leave our boards somewhere else, I offered.

Nah. It's cool. Really.

Okay, I said, unconvinced.

And listen, there's a little spurt of swell coming. Day after tomorrow, if it's blowing offshore, get up early.

Early?

Sparrowfart. I'll pick you both up. We'll go somewhere . . . discreet.

Secret.

Yeah. I think you're ready.

We trundled on up to my place and I climbed down and grabbed my bike. As I pedalled up the choppy drive in the last light of day I could hear the VW labouring back out of town towards the coast, and the sound of it still clattered through the trees when I reached the house in its tufty paddock and its aura of roasting smells and radio.

The next day Loonie and I had a job pulling down a shed behind the butcher's, and while we twisted out nails with pinch bars and claw hammers, I tried to engage him in speculation about Eva and Sando. Personally I found the tears and arguments enthralling. Nobody blued like that over at my place and it was as exciting as it was disconcerting. I was curious about what it was between them that set them off, but I couldn't interest Loonie in anything beyond Eva's many shortcomings. He saw the whole scene as evidence that she was nothing but a stuck-up pain in the arse. She was a drag, a bitch, a stupid Yank, and a junkie.

Painkillers, my arse, he said.

But, what about that limp? There's something wrong with her.

Yeah, she's a whingein female.

Still, I said. You notice how she always wears jeans? You reckon people still get polio in America?

Jesus, who cares? I wish she'd go back there.

She's not that bad.

You saw those mags. He was famous, mate, and maybe if it wasn't for her he still would be. Chicks, Pikelet. They drag you down.

I thought you fancied her, I ventured.

You're full of shit.

I let it go and kept working in the grit and mildew of the old shed. I knew I was on dangerous ground here with Loonie, yet his bluster made me smile because I'd seen him look at her – all those sidelong glances, the way he took in the heavy swing of her braid and the solid curve of her breast – but since the day she drove us back in the rain, his dislike had been implacable. It was as if his contempt for her fuelled his devotion to Sando. For in Loonie's mind, Eva would always be the millstone around our hero's neck. Her smooth American skin and blue eyes seemed to enrage him. He hated her acerbic talk and slanting mouth. She was in his way. She always stood between him and Sando and she knew it, came to enjoy the fact.

Eva was right about Sando and us. The box of magazines had surely been some sort of provocation, one of many things that were never really explained. Later I wondered if she'd done it to make him see what was developing between him and two boys less than half his age, to give him pause. I can't pretend to know what effect the gesture had on Sando, or how they settled it between them, if they ever did at all, but I know that those photos only served to increase our awe of him. Years on I had time enough and cause to wonder if she'd really had other, murkier motives, thoughts she didn't admit to or yet understand.

Sando pulled up at dawn with a dinghy hitched to the Volksie. It was the first Saturday of the new year. So began what he called our appointments with the undisclosed. We were, he said in a slightly thespian manner, gentlemen in search of a discreet location, and we understood, without his having to say a word, that we were also now a secret society of three.

He drove us west through miles and miles of forest. Morning light fell across the road in webs and in time we came to a small, unfamiliar bridge where Sando swung off onto a side track which led to the bank of a deep creek. Nonplussed as we were, Loonie and I did what we were told and helped guide the trailer and dinghy to the water's edge. The boat was loaded with fuel and three boards much longer and narrower than our own. When our eyes met across the gunwales Loonie broke into his split-lip grin.

We wound down the creek through a tunnel of overhanging trees until it met a broad estuary whose shores were densely timbered. There were no huts or jetties here, nothing to suggest that people came by at all, and it was obvious that none of this country had ever been logged. The landscape looked primeval.

Sando throttled up and sent us charging across the shallow inlet. When I glanced back at him in the stern, clinging to the tiller with the wind furrowing his hair and beard, his smile was cryptic, even sly.

At the plugged mouth of the river the estuary narrowed to a little cul-de-sac between high, marbled dunes and on the seaward side there was a high bar like the one at Sawyer Point. When Sando killed the motor we heard the rumble of surf but we couldn't yet see the ocean.

Where are we? asked Loonie.

This is Barney's, said Sando, already reaching for his wetsuit. This whole stretch of coast sticks out further south than anywhere, so it picks up every bit of swell.

How come the name? I asked.

Cause Barney lives here, he said with that fey grin.

Loonie and I both looked about. There was still no

sign of habitation, no footprints in the sand, not even a vehicle track in the hills beyond.

Only fair to tell you, said Sando.

Lives where? said Loonie scornfully.

Sando cocked his head seaward and stood up in the boat to pull on his suit. He stepped out and we followed his lead. We helped pull the dinghy onto the sand then took up the boards he assigned us and followed him up onto the buttress of the bar where we finally saw the long sweep of the bay.

Oh, man, said Loonie. Far out.

I stared at the clean, blue walls of swell fanning down the empty beach. Each wave broke about two hundred yards out at an angle to the shore and peeled evenly east across the sandbanks into the tiny distance. I couldn't believe how long the wave was, and as if reading my thoughts, Sando explained that it was best to walk back up the beach after each ride. There was not a human mark on the beach, only wheeling birds, seaspray and the white noise of falling water.

And what about Barney? I asked with a misplaced grin, assuming that I was up with the joke.

He's not hungry all the time, said Sando. Which improves the odds.

Fuck, said Loonie. Tell me it's not a shark.

Okay. It's not a shark.

Loonie gave out a wheezy laugh of relief, and I laughed along with him.

Well, said Sando. Not your *average* shark, put it that way.

The laughter died in our throats.

It's not that big a deal. I've been comin here for years and look at me. Still got all me fingers and toes.

But you've *seen* it? I croaked.

Oh, yeah. Five, six times.

And what kind of bloody shark is this? said Loonie hotly.

Like I said. Not your average noah.

Stop pissin about and just say it, said Loonie.

He's a white pointer, mate. The great white hunter.

Fuck! Fuckin fuck!

Now you can shit yourself all you want. Pants down, son, knock yourself out.

Sando and Loonie stood there, staring each other down. You just didn't call Loonie out like that. I knew he wouldn't take a backward step now, not for man nor boy. I shrank back, feeling like the bird-chested kid that I was, and waited for something to blow.

How big is this thing? I asked, as if it made a ghost of a difference.

Aw, maybe fourteen foot, said Sando genially enough. He still had Loonie in a steely glare. Hard to tell, Pikelet. Got a big ole head, though, and a grin like Richard-fuckin-Nixon.

So – I was desperate for diversion now – why's he called Barney?

Sando laughed. I named him after Eva's old man; he thinks I'm a waste of skin. He won't eat me outright, the father-in-law, but he likes to show the ivories every now and then, just to remind me who's boss. So, Barney it is. Come on, let's hit it while the tide's in.

Loonie threw down his board. Why the fuck you bring us here for?

Make men of you, said Sando. Thought you had the nads for it. Coupla giant-killers like yourselves. Boys who say they surf Outside Point at eight feet.

We bloody did, said Loonie. And there's witnesses.

So you say. And maybe you did. But, gosh, Loon. Weren't you *scared*?

Piss off.

Hell, I was, I muttered.

Least you're honest, Pikelet. But scared of what? Water over sand? A bit of a sinus-flush? What's to be scared of out there at the Point?

It was bloody eight foot, said Loonie. Ten!

Sando just snorted. He turned and jogged down to the water's edge and launched himself into the deep, moiling gutter of the rip. We watched him pick his way to the deep channel that ran out to the break, paddling casually, duckdiving spills of whitewater and shaking spray from his hair.

It's all bullshit, said Loonie. He's shittin us.

I shrugged.

He's callin us fuckin sooks.

Maybe, I said.

Thinks we're just gunna sit here like a coupla girls.

Girls or no girls, I was quite prepared to do exactly that, to sit there safe and warm on the beach and watch Sando dice it out with Barney. I was already thinking about what to do if he was eaten, whether I could remember how to start the outboard. Driving the Kombi home presented a few problems, but I figured I'd tackle these lesser obstacles one at a time. But before I could get anything straight in my mind Loonie took up his board with a strangled, angry cry and ran down to the water. A few moments later, hapless and terrified, I followed him.

That's how we surfed Barney's the first time, with Loonie taking on every wave enraged, and me just trailing along, dry-mouthed and shaky, until the exhilaration of the rides themselves inoculated us both against the worst of our fear.

The wave at Barney's wasn't huge but it was long and perfect: blue, pure, and empty. It was like something from a magazine and we were in it. Loonie and I strove to outdo each other, to take off as late as possible, to drop in with the kind of studied nonchalance we copied from Sando, and then steer up into the shimmering cave each wave made of itself. Inside those waves our voices bounced back at us, deeper and larger for all the noise, like the voices of men. We felt strong, older. We came howling from the gullet of wave upon wave and stopped believing in the shark altogether. It was a landmark day.

We surfed Barney's for months with Sando before the secret got out. Some nosy crew from Angelus followed us in, saw the tyre tracks and found the parked VW and trailer. But even when they showed up, more surfers watched from the beach than actually paddled out. Especially after the spring morning when Barney surfaced like a sub in the channel, rolled over beside Loonie and fixed him with one terrible, black eye before sliding away again.

That eye, said Loonie, was like a fuckin hole in the universe.

It was as close as he got to poetry. I envied him the moment and the story that went with it.

Heading home from that first day at Barney's, bone-sore and lit up, we relived the morning wave by wave, shoring it up against our own disbelief. By common assent, Loonie had caught the wave of the day. It was a smoker. I was paddling back out through the channel when he got to his feet. The wave reared up, pitched itself forward and simply swallowed him. I heard him scream for joy or terror and could only see him intermittently as he navigated a path beneath the warping fold of water. He was a blur in there, ghostly. When finally he shot out and passed me, he looked back at the weird, dilating eye of the wave and gave it the finger.

Geez, I wish we had a camera, he said afterwards, as we chugged back through the forest. It was too good. Shoulda got a photo.

Nah, said Sando. You don't need any photo.

But just to show, to prove it, sorta thing.

You don't have to prove it, said Sando. You were there.

Well, least you blokes saw it.

My oath, I said.

But it's not even about us, said Sando. It's about you. You and the sea, you and the planet.

Loonie groaned. Hippy-shit, mate.

Is that right? said Sando indulgently.

Orright for you. You got plenty of shots to prove what you done. Honolua Bay, man. Fuckin A.

All that's just horseshit, said Sando. It's wallpaper.

Easy for you to say.

Sando was quiet for a moment. You'll learn, he said in the end.

Loonie beat his chest there in the confines of the Kombi cab.

Learn? Mate, I bloody *know*!

I laughed but Sando was unmoved.

Son, he said. Eventually there's just you and it. You're too busy stayin alive to give a damn about who's watchin.

Mate, said Loonie, straining to maintain his bravado. I don't know what language you're talkin.

You'll be out there, thinkin: am I gunna die? Am I fit enough for this? Do I know what I'm doin? Am I solid? Or am I just . . . ordinary?

I stared, breathless, through the broken light of trees.

That's what you deal with in the end, said Sando. When it's gnarly.

How does it feel? I murmured.

How does what feel?

When it's that serious.

You'll find out.

Like, I mean, twenty feet, said Loonie subdued now.

Well, you're glad there's no stupid photo. When you make it, when you're still alive and standin at the end, you get this tingly-electric rush. You feel *alive,* completely awake and in your body. Man, it's like you've felt the hand of God. The rest of it's just sport'n recreation, mate. Give me the hand of God any day.

Shoulder to shoulder in the cab, Loonie and I exchanged furtive looks. There was something of the classroom about Sando, the stink of chalk on him when he got going, but my mind was racing. I'd already begun to pose those questions to myself and feel the undertow of their logic. Was I serious? Could I do something gnarly, or was I just ordinary? I'll bet my life that despite his scorn Loonie was doing likewise. We didn't know it yet, but we'd already imagined ourselves into a different life, another society, a state for which no raw boy has either words or experience to describe. Our minds had already gone out to meet it and we'd left the ordinary in our wake.

I DID MY SHARE of whining when the new school year began, but in truth I didn't really mind going back. There was no more swell that summer, no opportunity to test myself any further, and the days began to hang heavy. Within a week of the term commencing, I rediscovered the aisles and recesses of the Angelus school library. There was nothing like it in Sawyer and the only other collection of books I'd seen was out at Sando's. During my first year of high school I'd turned to reading as a kind of refuge, but that second year it became a pleasure in its own right.

I started with Jack London because I recognized the name from Sando's shelves. After I saw Gregory Peck gimping across the poop deck on telly I tried *Moby Dick*, though I can't say I got far. I found books on Mawson and Shackleton and Scott. I read accounts of Amundsen's race south against the English and the ruthlessness that made all the difference. I tried to imagine the Norwegian eating the very dogs that hauled him to the Pole – something harsh and bracing about the idea appealed to me. I read about British commandos, the French Resistance, about the specialized task of bomb disposal. I found Cousteau and then mariner-authors who recreated the voyages of the ancients in craft of leather and bamboo. I read about Houdini and men who had themselves shot from cannons or tipped in barrels over Niagara Falls. I fed on lives that were not at all ordinary, about men who in normal domestic circumstances might be viewed as strange, reckless, unbalanced. When I failed to get more than sixteen pages into *The Seven Pillars of Wisdom* I thought the failure was mine.

It was there in the stacks that I met the girl who decided without consultation that I was her boyfriend. She was a farm girl from further out east and she boarded at the dreaded hostel. Like me, she came to the library to escape, but she was already bookish. Her name was Queenie. She was handsome and wheat-haired, with the slightly intimidating shoulders of a competitive swimmer, and there was plenty about her to like, yet I suspect I only really liked her because she liked me first. Although I did very little to encourage such baffling interest, I somehow got used to it, and even came to expect it. She slagged off at my books of manly derring-do while I razzed her for her taste in stories about crippled girls overcoming cruel odds with the aid of improbably gifted animals.

At lunchtimes we didn't hang out so much as maintain a steady orbit in the library and even if we didn't have much to say we were never far away from one another. About a month into term, when the class had decided, as these things went in those days, that Queenie and I were an official couple, two army cadets from the year ahead of us made the general announcement, at full military volume, to the entire non-fiction section of the library, that Queenie Cookson had great tits. Whereupon the poor kid bolted to the toilet, leaving me in the care of a book about Helen Keller. I felt my face go hot – from recognition rather than shame – for those pillocks were, in their brutal way, completely correct about something I'd barely noticed. Yes, Queenie Cookson did have great tits and this was news confounding enough in itself, but how was I meant to react to it being broadcast like this in the library? Should I stand up and defend the girl's honour and then fight my way to the door, or kick back and leer in the reflected glory? Neither was really my style. I just sat there, blushing, while it slowly became evident that Queenie wouldn't be back soon. Even as I set aside Helen Keller and returned as casually as I could to the legless exploits of Douglas Bader, I knew I'd failed a test whose rules I didn't yet understand.

IN THE EARLY AUTUMN, just as the first good southerly swells arrived, Loonie broke his arm. We were farting about at a place called the Holes which was halfway along the cliffs to Old Smoky, and Loonie had spent the morning daring me to dare him to have himself shot from a blowhole like some mad adventurer from one of my books. He'd perfected his badgering technique. He worked on you so long and so consistently that out of rage and frustration you'd find yourself challenging him to do something you had no interest in him doing. Moreover, you ended up daring him with a passion that was, by this late stage, real enough to cause him genuine offence and so his indignation spurred him on to be even more stupid and dangerous than he intended.

Having yourself blasted from a blowhole is more silly than perilous and ours was a pretty naff effort. Thankfully, there weren't openings out there large enough for Loonie to climb right into; he had to settle for sitting across a foot-wide aperture to see what happened. All along that basalt shelf above the sea the blowholes sucked and gurgled around us, and each time a wave slammed in at the base of the cliffs there was an ominous lull before every crack and hole began to moan. When a good set hit the underbelly of the cliff the sudden blasts of spume could set you back in your tracks. The vapour had a nightmare stink. I kept well clear, fearful of the backdraught. I couldn't bear to think of being sucked down a black throat into the pounding guts of the caves below. I figured I'd rather be eaten alive by Barney.

In the end, Loonie's misadventure was more undignified than death-defying. He saddled up with a sick grin and instead of being hoisted skyward, he was spat across the rocks horizontally. He came directly at me, legs pedalling, shirt blown fat as a lifejacket, and with all that snowy hair in his eyes he couldn't see where he was headed. I dropped. He caught his foot in the leg of my shorts and slammed down on the rock with twice the force he'd begun with. When he got up his arm was all wrong. It was a hard trek back to the Point.

We were lucky Eva was home. She saved me from having to wheel Loonie all the way back to town on my bike. He fainted twice in the cab of the VW and Eva tried not to appear as though she was enjoying his spells.

Barely three weeks later it was this fracture that prevented him from surfing Old Smoky. It changed things between us in ways we could neither foresee nor understand.

During the summer just gone, while we'd chafed at the chance to prove ourselves, the ocean went flat. We dived with Sando more than we got to surf with him. On breathless-hot days he took us out around the Point to remote groper holes along the cliffs. These trips were designed to test our lung capacity more than anything but we loved to hunt for food. We swam into deep granite crevices to pull abalone with Sando at our side, deeper with every dive, and often as not we outlasted him. I couldn't tell if Sando was simply letting us best him for reasons of his own, but Loonie and I had trained ourselves to really soak the goodness from a lungful of air. When it came to freediving we knew what we were doing, and going for abalone was infinitely more fun than lying on the black bottom of the river with your arms wrapped around a slimy tree root. The sea was brimming with stuff to help you forget the pain in your chest. It was worth the spotted vision and the roar in your skull to be able to chase a big blue groper into its lair. Some days we'd hike back across the ridge with a fifty-pound fish and a bag of abalone and spend the afternoon filleting and shucking in the shade of Sando's killing tree. While we worked we pestered him into telling us about Old Smoky. At first he was evasive about the bombora, but we kept at him until he gave up tidbits of information in his cagey, elliptical way; it was maddening, but it charmed us.

Right from the get-go Loonie was desperate to surf Old Smoky. He believed he was ready. I wasn't so sure I was up to it. The reef was a mile out to sea on a lonely, wild bit of coast, and from what I'd seen the wave itself was huge. Whenever there was a swell big enough to make it break properly you couldn't launch a boat within twenty miles, so the only approach was to bash out across the bush track from the Point to the cliffs, and crab your way down the rock-face until you got within jumping range. We were supposed to launch ourselves off the storm-swept cliff. And then you began the mile-long paddle out to sea. I dreaded it, was tantalized by the prospect, and the worse Sando made it sound, the harder it was to resist the thought.

When he knew we were hooked Sando stopped being coy. He brought out marine charts of the area to show how the seabed rose from the continental shelf, how drastic the bathymetry was at Old Smoky where water simply reared up on the shoal and turned itself inside out. He drew diagrams of the set-up for us, the landmarks to navigate by to find the impact zone and the safety of the deep channel beside it. It's a pretty simple affair, really, he told us. Once you choose the right wave you're halfway home, but if you judge wrong, if you take off from too far across the reef, then you're in more trouble than the early settlers.

Then he took us out there. It was a baking February day. The ocean was a mirror. From just beneath Sando's place we boated down the estuary, hauled the dinghy up over the bar and launched out into the placid bay where we skated around the Point and headed west to the cliff-coast beyond. The sea-torn footings of the bluffs were tranquil, the blowholes dormant.

When we got out to Old Smoky conditions were so

calm there wasn't much to see from the boat. Sando confirmed the landmarks for us – the way the trees inland matched up with a streak of lime down the cliff inshore. The reef itself was only a dim shadow below.

Deep, I murmured.

Won't seem so deep from the top of a twenty-footer, said Sando. Let's see how deep. May as well do our homework.

We dropped the anchor in the purple water of the channel and ten fathoms of rope snaked out before it found bottom. Wc had only masks and no fins. We watched Sando plunge in and swim over to the reef. Loonie and I hit the water a moment later.

Rising sharply from the seabed the shoal at Old Smoky was like a sunken building, windows open, teeming with blue morwongs, harlequins and boarfish. In the water column above, schools of buffalo bream churned restless circles. Because Sando was watching and because we could, we speared past him for the bottom, to make solid the idea of the place and the stories we fed on. We kicked down barefoot and shaped ourselves to glide, purging as we went. In the mouths of caves were lobsters the size of cattle dogs. At thirty feet I took a handhold in the rock and rolled over to see Sando as a black star up there at the surface. Loonie slid down beside me and hooked on.

We hung there for the longest time, the two of us, locked in the old rivalry, smiling madly, around our snorkels while the sea clicked and rattled around us. Fish arrived, curious at first and then anxious when we showed no sign of moving on. In time they fled into the blips and specks at the edges of my vision.

The first big cold fronts arrived while the water was still warm. For the best part of a fortnight we pored over forecast maps, watching a chain of sub-Antarctic storms, hoping one might wander north towards us, or that two might converge and peel away in our direction to bring the sort of weather required to make Old Smoky break. Sando told us that the best of the groundswell would arrive before the storm-fronts themselves, that waves were little more than lines of energy from events beyond the horizon. I tried to imagine them, these radiating shocks, as they rolled toward us like harbingers of a trouble we couldn't yet see. Along with Loonie I was excited and jittery, though there was still something unreal about the rigmarole of preparation when the storms themselves seemed so abstract.

In these weeks before Easter Sando was solemn and pensive. We'd pedal out to his place only to sit on the steps for an hour while he went through his yoga routine and Eva glowered at us from the open doorway. We did our best not to pester him. We knew that he drove out along the ridges with his binoculars every day, that he was watching and waiting while we were in school, and we saw that he had huge, pointed big-wave boards laid out in readiness beneath the house. There was nothing left to do but wait.

My parents wouldn't have had any idea about what I was preparing for. I can only assume that they accepted my story about Sando, who was, I said, just a bloke who gave Loonie and me a lift now and then, someone for whom we did odd jobs. Whether or not they believed this story, they never challenged me over it. They were not suspicious like Loonie's old man. He had Sando and Eva pegged as layabouts and drug-addled hippies and he'd already forbidden his son from going out to their place, but Loonie – who was always good at covering his tracks and an excellent liar besides – had never been the sort of boy who felt compelled to do as he was told. He regularly slept at our place on weekends. For all his sly grins I knew he liked the homely manner in which my parents did things. He even liked the mortifying way my mother would come into my room some nights to try to tuck us into our beds. It was, I suppose, a taste of the domestic life he'd missed out on, though at times he seemed to be play-acting. Being with us a few days a week meant he could escape his father's brutal moods, but it was also a means of avoiding surveillance, for Sando had long been in the habit of picking us both up from my house.

Had my parents known what Sando was actually getting me into, I doubt they would have been so trusting. Back then, the idea of a grown man spending so much time with teenaged boys wouldn't have troubled them or anybody else, for all that sort of fear and panic was far in the future, but knowing that he was training us to go to sea to leap from the cliffs in a storm swell and put ourselves in harm's way would have been something else entirely. Perhaps it was irresponsible of Sando to lead us into such a situation. At that age we were physically undeveloped, too small to safely manage what we set out to do, and he did it without our parents' consent. I have no doubt that in a later era he'd have been seen as reckless and foolhardy, yet when you consider the period and the sorts of activities that schools and governments sanctioned, Sando's excursions seem like small beer. We could have been staying back at school as army cadets, learning to fire mortars and machine-guns, to lay booby traps and to kill strangers in hand-to-hand combat like other boys we knew, in preparation for a manhood that could barely credit the end of the war in Vietnam. Sando appealed to one set of boyish fantasies and the state exploited others. Eva was right – we were Sando's wide-eyed disciples – but in the sixties and seventies when we were kids there were plenty of other cults to join, cults abounding.

AS IT HAPPENED Sando came for us while Loonie's arm was still in plaster.

We woke in the night to the booming swell but neither of us said anything. If tomorrow was the day then only one of us would be paddling out with Sando. Once awake we lay silent for hours and when we heard the VW come threshing up the inlet road, we dressed quickly and crept from the house. But at the end of the boggy drive where the Kombi sputtered and chugged, Loonie veered off into the dark street.

What's he up to? yelled Sando, cranking a window down.

I shrugged, but I already knew.

Doesn't he even wanna watch?

No, I said. He doesn't.

Here, get in.

We puttered up behind Loonie with the windows down. The air was freezing and nobody in Sawyer seemed to be up.

Hey, Loonie, said Sando as we eased alongside to keep pace with him. Aren't you gonna come and watch out for your mate?

What for? said Loonie. Spoil ya secret hippy moment?

Don't be a dickhead. C'mon, watch and learn.

Oh, no fuckin worries. I'd love that.

Least you could show your mate a bit of support.

What for? He's chicken.

Jesus, son. Don't be an arsehole.

Fuck off, coach.

Sando gave a bitter, disappointed laugh, but Loonie kept walking. I thought Sando might persist a little, cajole him, but he wound the window up and pulled away. At first I was stunned but after a few moments the humiliation of it sank in. Loonie was right. He knew I wasn't up to it. Still, I couldn't believe he'd come out and say it like that, in front of Sando. I craned back for a glimpse of his white hair, but he was gone in the gloom. There were three boards strapped to the rear tray. They were Brewers, huge beautiful things. Three of them. As though Sando had brought an extra as a gesture for Loonie's sake.

I *am* chicken, I said.

Oh, fuck, said Sando. Everyone's chicken. That's why we do this silly shit.

You reckon?

Yeah, to face it down, mate. To feel it, eat it. And shit it out with a big hallelujah.

He laughed. And I laughed because he did, to hide my fear.

When we hauled up past the Point the bay was awash with foam and shrouded with vapour. The surge of the shorebreak overran the ramparts of the bar and spewed into the estuary. The ocean sounded like a battlefield; the unceasing roar was audible even above the sound of the Volkswagen.

Sando nursed the vehicle up the tracks and out to the last ridge. It was slow going but I wasn't in a hurry. When he switched the engine off the noise of the sea was frightening. He took up the binoculars while I peered southward through the dawn light. Beyond the turmoil at the base of the cliffs the ocean was strangely smooth. There was still a faint offshore breeze at our backs, meaning the storms themselves were still a day away. The first sun gave the water a benign sheen and for a few minutes there was nothing much to see, little enough for a swoon of relief to course through me. I was, I thought, off the hook. And then a mile out I saw the sudden white flare. A plume of spray lifted off the bommie like the dust kicked up by a convoy of log-trucks and after a second's delay the sound of it reached us. Now that was a noise to snap a boy out of his dreamy sense of wellbeing.

Well, Pikelet, said Sando. Looks like we'll get wet this morning.

I could barely carry that yellow Brewer. It was ten feet long and wouldn't fit under my skinny arm so I balanced it on my head the way the old-timers did in the days of balsa boards and Gidget and D-fins. The heath around us was filled with peppery smells and alive with the nip and dash of honeyeaters. We hiked west to where all the boulders were whiskered with lichen. I followed Sando. We didn't say much. I watched the muscles flex in his bare back. The wetsuit was shucked down to his waist and its neoprene arms flapped against his thighs.

It was a half-hour walk. I was so troubled about Loonie that for whole minutes at a time I forgot to be afraid. Had it been me with the busted arm I'd have come to watch, out of gratitude for the let-off as much as from comradely feeling, and I certainly wouldn't have gone around calling anyone a chicken – nobody, not friend nor foe. I wasn't old enough then to know that you only call someone a coward from safe ground, fortified by the certainty of your own courage or by your deluded faith in it. But Loonie always had absolute self-assurance. There have been times since when I've thought of him as an endless and rather aimless reservoir of physical bravery, and that this defining characteristic distorted him somehow, keeping him from subtler feelings. In middle age I look back on Loonie with sad wonder. He was real enough, but less of a friend than I'd imagined, and perhaps that morning marked the beginning of my disaffection, for although I was in awe of him I hated him for saying what he said. Yet maybe I owed him a debt that day, for the longer I brooded on his outburst, hiking along the clifftops in Sando's wake, the angrier I got. It was this fury and little else that hardened my resolve and kept me from running away.

We picked our way down a scrubby, windswept slope where sea-mist rose in our faces and at a steep cliff we passed the boards down in stages until finally we stood on a tongue of rock above a surging gap. We shoved our sneakers into clefts above us, and all the time Sando spoke to me quietly, like a horse-breaker. Between incoming waves the gully beneath us emptied out to reveal a hanging garden of kelp and limpets. When the water returned, it surged green to just below where we stood. Now and then a wave sprawled right up the rock to explode in a mess of foam.

Getting off's the easy part, said Sando. Coming back in you'll have to concentrate. Time the surge and pick the biggest. Come in on the back of it. If you don't make it all the way up here you'll be stuck halfway and the next wave'll splatter you against the cliff. You gotta be patient, Pikelet. If it takes half an hour, that's what it takes, you hear?

I nodded. My right leg shook; it felt unconnected to

the rest of my body. The size of the waves, the length of the paddle, the monumental shadow of the cliff – everything was beyond imagining.

I watched Sando shrug into the top half of his wetsuit and take up his big orange Brewer. He pinched my cheek and grinned. The sun shone in his beard and in his eyes, and his teeth were strong and white.

You still wanna do this?

I no longer trusted myself to speak. I just took up my board beside him and stood shivering in my shorts.

Shit, he said as a great, green glut of water poured up at our feet. I wonder what the ordinary people are doin today.

With that, while the sea was all but upon us, he launched out with his board like a shield before him and landed smoothly and paddled briskly with the receding surge. In a moment he was out in deep water beyond the turbulence.

I looked down into the maw and waited for the surge to return. Sando sat up to wait. Birds shrieked behind me. The rocks streamed with fizz. Every crack spilled rivulets and streams and sheets until suddenly the sea came back and Sando started yelling and then I braced and jumped.

The paddle out was so long and disorientating that it became kind of abstract. I followed the cheesy, yellow soles of Sando's feet and fell into a rhythm. Half an hour later, still two hundred yards shy of the reef itself, I sat up beside him in a dreamy calm. Perhaps it was the warm sun and the exertion and the fact that we'd paddled out during a long lull, but I began to feel safe and happy. When the first wave broke over Old Smoky, all that equanimity simply evaporated.

We were in deep water, safe enough in the scheme of things, and I hadn't yet understood the scale of what I was seeing, but the sight of the thing pitching out across the bommie drove a blade of fear right through me. Just the sound of spray hissing back off the crest inspired terror; it was the sound of sheetmetal shearing itself to pieces. The wave drove onto the shoal and the report cannoned across the water and slapped against my chest.

Sando hooted. He raised his arms to it and tossed his head back. The wave sprawled and growled and finally spat its wind into the pacifying depth of the channel so that by the time it reached us it was just a massive current with a trailing scum of spindrift.

Got your bearings?

Yeah, I lied.

Had I the slightest idea of where to go, I would have paddled straight back to the cliffs and climbed out right then. But behind me the land was featureless, just a grey-black slab which disappeared between swells.

Sando paddled on up to the channel in tight to the

reef where the swells humped prodigiously but did not quite break. At a loss and scared of being alone, I followed. He paddled and propped, paddled and propped, checking and adjusting his position all the time. He motioned me closer as a fresh set lumbered in. At first all I saw was a series of dark lines in the distance and then these swells became a convoy, bearing down on us, increasing in size and speed with every passing moment until they became distinct waves that warped and wedged so massively that I found myself looking uphill into great sunstruck ridges. You could feel the whole skin of the ocean being drawn outward to meet them, and it was impossible to resist the conviction that we were about to be mown down, even here in the safe depth of the channel.

We sat tight while four waves went by. Then Sando paddled over and put himself in harm's way. I stayed out wide; I wasn't going anywhere. He rose, still sitting, over the next wave, lifted into the sky without expression, and for a long time afterwards he was obscured by spray. When I saw him next he was stroking into the path of the biggest wave I'd ever seen. As the thing drew itself up onto the reef, he seemed, for all his beetling, to be sucked back up its lumpy slope. A moment later the wave broke, spangled and streaked and pluming vapour behind him, and he was up, falling bent-legged into the pit below. Despite the surface chop he kept his feet to come sweeping down from three storeys high and when he ploughed by I caught a jaunty flash of teeth and saw he was okay.

When he paddled back out Sando was singing. He slapped water my way and did his best to unseat me. His eyes glittered; he was as lit up as I'd ever seen him.

Jesus, he said laughing. God! You gotta get some of that.

Just watchin, I said, panting with anxiety.

Aw!

Yeah, I said. Really.

Doesn't come around every week, mate.

No.

Never forgive yourself.

Maybe, I said breathless.

I think you're ready, Pikelet.

Hm.

I shook my head and bobbed dumbly out there in the purple-deep ocean with a bitter taste in my mouth.

Mountains of water rose from the south; they rumbled by, gnawing at themselves, spilling tons of foam, and the half-spent force of them tore at my dangling legs. There was just so much water moving out there, such an overload of noise and vibration; everything was at a scale I couldn't credit. I began to hyperventilate. Only later could I appreciate how alert Sando was that morning. Though he sensed my panic he did not touch me. Had he even got up close, or tried to grab my board and reassure me I'd have lashed out. I was wild with fear and we were a mile out to sea, the two of us, and now things had really gotten dangerous. But he knew what he was doing.

Tell you what, he said. Let's take a break. We don't have to do this. We'll try something different.

I didn't look at him. I couldn't shift my gaze from the horizon. We were in a lull now, but that was no comfort. I sensed him paddling east but I kept looking south as though my neck was locked in position. He was gone; he was nowhere near the reef. And I was alone. On my own. The body understood before my mind caught up. I forced myself to snatch a glimpse. Sando was more than fifty yards off. He was right over in the safe deep away from the reef and he was waving and calling. There was nothing urgent in his tone. He sounded positively languid. I heard a calming authority in his voice, a familiarity that tugged at me. He looked so secure and comfortable sitting up with his hands on his thighs and his elbows out like muttonbird wings, and I felt doubly exposed out there by the break. I was caught. I stared back out to sea. I doubted I could move. Sando kept up some sort of banter across the distance, while the fear boiled up in me. I heard how nasty and ragged my breathing had become. I was lightheaded. And then, quite suddenly, I was too afraid to stay there. It was as if I'd pitched up against my own panic and bounced back. I swung the board his way, dropped flat and began to paddle. When I got there I was gasping.

Let's dive, he said casually. I'll beat you to the bottom.

Without another word he stood up on his Brewer and speared into the water between us. I sat up in a funk, alone again. I couldn't bear it; he must have known I'd follow him.

It was too deep out there to see the sandy bottom, especially without a mask, but I could dimly make out the soles of Sando's feet as he kicked down. I clawed after him and, after a few moments, settled into a steep, calming glide. I was already oxygen-soaked from all the hyperventilation and I didn't have the buoyancy of a wetsuit to contend with, so I caught up with him quickly enough, and within a few seconds I overtook him. Blood drummed at my temples. My chest felt as if it would implode. Every bubble tore at me. I felt like a dying comet. When I finally ran out of speed and conviction I levelled off, and when I looked up I saw Sando's blurry outline at some distance. Down here the sea was its usual quiet self, all sleepy-dim and familiar. Some kind of animal recognition jolted me back into myself. It was only the sea, the water. Didn't I know what to do underwater? Slowly, returning with the burning need to breathe, came the old confidence. I knew what I was doing. I had control. I saw Sando's hazy thumbs-up and pumped back toward the surface. We rose together in our cauls of fizz and light and when we hit the air a few yards from our floating boards a surge of heat went through me and I knew I was okay.

That day I went back across to the bombora and rode two waves. Together those rides wouldn't add up to more than half a minute of experience, of which I can only recall a fraction: flickering moments, odd details. Like the staccato chat of water against the board. A momentary illusion of being at the same level as the distant cliffs. The angelic relief of gliding out onto the shoulder of the wave in a mist of spray and adrenaline. Surviving is the strongest memory I have; the sense of having walked on water.

Sando paddled up and held my hand like a brother or a father and I was babbling. I felt immortal and he just laughed. But already I wanted more. I was hankering for a third ride, something to make it real.

I sat for a few minutes while Sando took the next wave. He made it look easy and suddenly it did feel easy. I couldn't even wait for him to paddle back over. I paddled up to the impact zone and in a moment of overblown confidence put myself in the path of something the size of the Angelus town hall. I didn't understand how wildly I'd overreached until the moment I got to my feet and felt the whole edifice bulge and mutate beneath me.

For half a second I saw the shadow of the reef far below. The heavy board fell from under me like a leaf and I sprawled down the hard, unyielding face without it, bouncing from hip to hip, unable to break the skin of the water. I was falling down a staircase – one that never seemed to end, which collapsed on me and shot me skyward before snatching me down again so its rubble-spill might drive me headlong across the reef, rattling and wracking me all the way. I bounced and pinged and shot, winded and half blind, across the shoal, and when the reef fell away the turbulence ploughed me so deep and so fast I barely had a chance to equalize to save my eardrums. I knew not to fight it, but I was nearly gone when the sea let me go. I came up choking, sobbing, kicking at the surface as though I could climb into purer oxygen.

By the time Sando reached me I'd regained some composure but he'd seen it all. I was two hundred yards from where I'd caught the wave and my shorts were gone entirely.

Well, he said with a grin. That one rang your bell.

He pulled me onto his Brewer and said nothing about my bare arse. My board lay bright in the distance. He let me lie there a while before he swam off to get it and when he came back he called it a day. I paddled in after him and hoped there had been no witnesses.

We didn't go looking for Loonie that afternoon, but we knew he'd show up eventually. Eva fed us fish burgers and let us prattle until fatigue overtook us and we lapsed into stupefied silence. As the storm-front darkened the sky, we hung in hammocks on the verandah where the wind was eerie-warm. I was sore and so drowsy I kept falling asleep. The sound of magpies and wattlebirds was a conversation going over my head, a kind of chatter I felt I'd understand if only I kept swimming up from sleep towards wakefulness.

Later in the day the dog barked and Loonie came stumping along the rutted drive. It was raining by then. He pushed the dog away and hesitated before coming across the yard to the verandah steps. The plaster cast was slung like a weapon across his chest.

Come on, called Sando. Get outta the rain.

Loonie just stood there.

Don't be such a goddamn punk, said Eva, swinging out of her hammock.

She stared at him a moment, hands on hips, before limping inside, and only then did Loonie come upstairs to stand against the verandah rail. His sunbleached hair was flat on his skull and the calico sling wet through.

Eva came back with a towel. He took it without acknowledging her.

Well? he said.

Eva snorted and went inside. She closed the French doors a tad too firmly. Sando considered Loonie for some moments and then lay back to swing a bit. Loonie glanced at me. I averted my eyes.

All this time, said Sando. Surfing the place on my own. Watching it, biding my time, keeping my little secret. Funny, you know, but it was nice to share. A real surprise but it felt good. So maybe the best part about having a secret is letting someone in on it. Eh, Pikelet?

I shrugged, unable to keep from smiling.

How big?

Sando sighed. Big enough to make it interesting, he said. Big enough to rip the boy-wonder's shorts off.

Twenty foot, I said.

Fifteen, maybe. You rode it at fifteen, Pikelet, eighteen tops.

Well, he got waves, said Loonie dully.

Yeah, he made two. He did good.

Loonie stood there and took it in.

I shat meself, I said. I took the worst floggin. I freaked.

But he did the deed, said Sando. Made himself a little bit of history.

It took me a moment to absorb what he'd said. For if Sando was the first to have ridden Old Smoky, then I was surely the youngest. I could see Loonie thinking it through right there in front of me. He flapped the soggy hems of his jeans. The gesture was nonchalant, but I knew him better than that.

Your time'll come, said Sando.

Loonie shrugged, as if it was no big deal to him. But he was already making plans, I was sure of it. He'd seen what he had to do. He couldn't be the first or the youngest, so he'd have to go the hardest. He'd push it all the way.

There were only two more go-outs at Old Smoky that autumn, days when Loonie watched bitterly from the cliff, but by mid-winter he finally got his chance. He came with us on a grey, windless morning during a huge south-easterly swell when a skein of mist lay across the cliffs. Climbing down towards the water I heard voices and after leaping out and paddling clear I saw that a few of the Angelus crew had followed us. Loonie wanted an audience – he'd tipped them off – and although Sando said nothing as we stroked seaward, his anger was palpable. Loonie had really set himself a task.

But he set a new mark that day, no question about it. He did more than prove himself. He surfed like someone who didn't believe in death. The manic grin was gone. He clawed hungrily into the line-up and gave no quarter. It was twenty feet out there, maybe more, and he went later and deeper than either of us, never once begging off. He ploughed down those black-bellied monsters in a low crouch, his feet planted wide, while Sando and I sat in the channel and hooted in disbelief. Whatever we did that day, Loonie did it harder. I can't believe he wasn't afraid, but he had the cold determination of a boy completely overtaken by an idea. It wasn't that he was invulnerable or even particularly graceful, because he took some terrible beatings in attempting the impossible, but for every wave that nailed him he'd squeak clear of two others just as gnarly. He was fifteen years old. He hadn't simply taken Old Smoky on – he'd taken it over. From that day forward it was Loonie who set the benchmark. Sando and I could only watch in awe. And there, when we came in, was the Angelus crew, misted in on the cliff, uncertain of what it was they'd seen.

SO THERE WE WERE, this unlikely trio. A select and peculiar club, a tiny circle of friends, a cult, no less. Sando and his maniacal apprentices. Very few people ever really knew what we did out there along the cliffs; it was, after all, behaviour beyond the realms of logic. But within the tiny surfing fraternity along that part of the coast in those years we had a certain underground reputation. Bit by bit a special aura settled upon us and in our way we were rather solemn about what we did. Under Sando's tutelage we ate carefully and worked on our fitness. He taught us yoga. We grew stronger and more competent, expected more of ourselves and forsook almost everything else for the sake of the shared obsession. Years before people started speaking about extreme sports, we spurned the word *extreme* as unworthy. What we did and what we were after, we told ourselves, was the extraordinary.

Yet some reserve had set in alongside all this grand feeling. In the water with Sando, Loonie and I were part of a team so thoroughly coached and briefed that in big waves we could anticipate every move the other made. We saw bad falls coming and were ready to effect a rescue in a hold-down or in the event of injury, and this was comforting to know when you found yourself hurtling along beneath a thousand tons of whitewater, rag-dolling across the reef with your lungs near to bursting. In our boyish way we thought of it as a war zone out there on the bommies and we styled ourselves as comrades-under-fire. We were proud of our maverick status, even if it was semi-secret; we were into things that ordinary townsfolk could barely imagine. Sando was big on discretion. He did his best to instil in us a quiet sense of modesty. His hippified warrior spirit, so hard to grasp at this remove, was for a boy like me, basking in the glow of his authority, a code as tangible as it was heady.

Meanwhile a gap opened between Loonie and me. Those weeks he spent in plaster did the damage. His long, brooding wait as Sando and I surfed Old Smoky without him had curdled things between us, and it couldn't be undone. It was never sufficient for me to acknowledge his superior courage. He was the duck's nuts and I told him so. I didn't compete with him anymore because it was an unequal contest and I didn't need the grief. Yet I did secretly believe I had a style he lacked. Never a pretty surfer, Loonie was often a triumph of guts over technique. I didn't challenge him, but the struggle between us was never-ending, and out of the water things were definitely cooler.

Loonie's devotion to Sando grew more intense. For all his surliness and tough-guy scepticism, Loonie hurled himself at Sando like a son putting himself in his father's path. He became mulish about it; he liked to make things awkward. He often rode out to Sando's without me and routinely forgot to pass on his messages.

On the surface things appeared normal enough. In big surf we were still solid, but elsewhere, when Sando wasn't present to temper him, Loonie became less fun to be around. I didn't exactly avoid him; he often had other fish to fry. Between swells he ran with an older crew of Ag School boys, kids with stubbly chins and smokers' coughs. They bought the grog he swiped from the pub and they sold him detonators, .303 cartridges and stick mags in return. I knew he kept a kero tin full of contraband buried in the forest. He had the makings of pipe bombs out there, and money he looted from guest rooms and passed-out drunks. All winter he bristled and burned with a fury I didn't understand. Everything seemed to be *my* fault, so I didn't mind being out of his way.

There came a spring morning, a dark, rain-misted day on the Angelus road, when the school bus shuddered to an unscheduled halt. I stirred from my travelling stupor and looked up to see a hellish mess on the bend ahead. The bus chugged and rattled at the shoulder of the highway. The driver seemed to hesitate between backing up and jumping down to render aid. On the road before us a cattle truck lay on its side with the remains of a small car pressed into its underbelly. Steers writhed on the bitumen, bellowing, kicking, lashing their heads against the road. One hauled itself into the ditch, a hind leg trailing lifeless behind it. Blood ran thin and copious in the rain; it seemed to make the culvert weeds greener than they were and it trickled downhill towards us as the bus filled with murmurs and sobs.

A farm vehicle eased up behind the wreck and a man got out. The vehicle pulled away again in the direction of Angelus while the newly arrived man dodged scrabbling beasts to crawl up into the underbelly of the truck. Finally the bus driver cranked the door open and went out to help. I watched him go, hunching in the rain, pulling up his collar. There was something about the slack pace of his stride that inflamed me. I got to my feet and plunged down the steps and sprinted past him toward the twisted shambles. The bus driver shouted above the noise of maimed animals. The road was an obstacle course of lurching bodies, dark tongues, and lolling eyes. There was a horrible scrape of hoofs on the tarmac. The air stank of Oxo cubes and shit and spilled diesel.

When I reached the farmer he was tugging at the car door in his town clothes and all he could say was Jesus Christ, Jesus Christ, on and on, over and over. I saw that the driver was dead. The way her head tilted back on her forward-thrust body was all wrong. She was so hard up against the steering column that all my senses recoiled. Beside her, the man in the passenger seat licked his lips in slow motion. His eyes were tarred shut by blood oozing from a gouge in his forehead.

Then the bus driver came up behind us, saying: The truckie, the truckie's stuck.

I climbed the frame of the trailer chassis and groped along the wet, slippery bars of the cattle-cage towards the cab. I didn't trust the sagging front wheel for a perch, so I bellied out on the door and peered into the window beneath me like a diver looking into a reef hole. Barely a foot away, shivering in an army surplus jumper, and hanging in his seatbelt, was a big bloke with a beard and gold fillings. The window between us fogged up. I called down to him to open it, but he didn't seem to hear me. He just shook there, slowly obscured beneath the fogging, rain-pelted glass while I yelled until I was hoarse, and then the cops arrived with a rifle, and the fire truck was there, and someone much bigger hauled me down and gave me a steaming mug of Milo that I couldn't drink for the life of me.

That same night the old man drove me back into Angelus for the school social. Even though I'd asked Queenie Cookson I really didn't want to go anymore, but my mother insisted that I show for the girl's sake, to save her the shame of being stood up. So in I went, scrubbed up in a yellow bodyshirt and flared corduroys, while the old man whiled away the hours fishing for skippy off the town jetty.

On the drive over, even at the bend with its hail of windscreen glass and crushed vegetation, neither of us said a thing. When we got to the school gym in Angelus I mumbled thanks for the ride and sloped in.

Inside a band from the city played songs by The Sweet and Status Quo. The dim lights, the music and the sight of all my classmates in their best duds made everything unreal. I felt as though I wasn't properly there. The cavernous hall was full of competing perfumes. There was so much glitter and lipstick that everybody looked like strangers and it took me ten minutes to find Queenie over by the basement stairs.

Why didn't you tell me about this morning? she shouted close to my ear.

I shrugged.

I had to get it from Polly Morgan.

I shrugged again.

Is it true they both died?

That's what they're sayin on the radio.

You looked shocking today, she said. Why didn't you say anything? You should have told me. I don't get you.

There was nothing I could think to say in reply so I shrugged once more. She scowled. I put my arm around her and this seemed to placate her somewhat. Later we danced to Sherbert and AC/DC tunes and the conversations we had with others were mostly lip-reading. We wound up in the deep shadows of the basement stairwell, clinching and kissing abstractedly until the lights flickered and it was all over.

When I got in the car the old man looked haggard.

You stink of fish, I said.

And you smell like a girl.

We drove home in such a silence that I found myself fiddling noisily and pointlessly with the radio knobs. It annoyed the old man, but the agitation kept him from falling asleep at the wheel.

Back home my mother was still awake in her candlewick dressing gown.

You look handsome, love, she said.

I stood away from the sink while the old man wearily cleaned his fish. The stares of all those dead eyes made my gut flutter in a way that was new to me. When he opened their silver bellies I went to my room and did not sleep.

THERE WERE several major swells that year as big lows rode up out of the Roaring Forties, but we spent more time waiting for them, discussing them, imagining them, than riding them. Winter had its many interludes when for weeks on end the wind turned sideshore and brought swell in at hopeless angles, and there were days and days of dark, squally chop when the sea was a misery to behold.

I watched the weather maps and waited for Sando, perpetually in a state of anguished anticipation. Somehow I'd gotten used to a certain underlying level of fear. When it was gone I missed it. After a huge day at

Barney's or a rare session at Old Smoky I came home charged – the euphoria lasted for days. But when it dissipated I became restless, even anxious. I couldn't concentrate at school. Whenever I condescended to go fishing on the estuary, the old man complained that I twitched and jiggled like an alky, that I wrecked a good morning out.

I took to running in the forest. I rode out to the rivermouth and back flat-strap. I did what I could to wear myself out, but at night I still lay awake, turning, sighing, waiting.

At school Queenie Cookson passed a note, via intermediaries, to outline my many flaws (I was moody, selfish and inattentive) and notify me that I was, forthwith, relieved of my duties as boyfriend. I did my best to take it badly but in truth I was relieved.

In the troughs between big days, Loonie was infinitely more resourceful than me. Having been addicted to danger all his life he could always find a pulse-raising challenge. That year he drilled a peephole in the pressed-tin wall of the pub's storeroom and forged an entirely new means of putting himself in peril.

A woman called Margaret Myers began staying weekends in the pub. Reputedly from Sydney, she was about forty and rather tall. She was dark-haired and curvy, wore kaftans and beads and smoked clove cigarettes.

She was all out of sync for Sawyer, but she quickly became a regular. Loonie thought she was the most sociable woman he'd ever met, though this was before he realized that she was making a living upstairs in Room 6. During the hectic hours of the Sunday session, when it seemed that all hell was breaking loose down in the bar, he took to watching through his spyhole as she entertained her guests. He said he'd witnessed things that made his eyes sore, stuff you could barely credit. I took in every lurid detail, but I didn't really believe him. In this instance the facts didn't matter to me at all. Margaret Myers was such a fabulous creation and Loonie such a great bullshitter that the telling and the idea were satisfaction enough.

But Loonie, in his uncanny way, seemed to sense my unbelief. God knows, I never called him a liar – I wasn't stupid enough to fall for that. I didn't even press him for the more prosaic details of corroboration, stuff about the spyhole, the angle of view, the convenience of her using the same room each time, yet he called me on it anyway, for just as he had a native genius for manufacturing a physical challenge where there was none, Loonie could find an accusation in any endorsement, and before long, with barely a word on your part, he'd have himself wound into an indignant fury and you'd find you'd somehow dared him to prove himself. In the case of Room 6 there was only one way for Loonie to feel himself vindicated.

Which is how I came to be in that storeroom one day lifting a grey scab of Juicy Fruit from the pressed-tin wall with Loonie's breath hot and sour in my ear. I didn't really want to be there. The entire operation of getting from woodshed to laundry and then making the fraught bolt upstairs hardly seemed worth the risk. The room stank of mops and damp cardboard and my heart beat so hard it made me queasy. I was breathless and sweating and when I first leant against the metal wall my forehead slid off the mission-brown paint.

It turned out that the spyhole was hardly required to prove Loonie's point. The squeak of the bed next door, the slap of meat and the low growls coming through the wall were evidence enough. But that bit of gum was a provocation. I peeled it off, pressed my eye to the gap and let out a grunt of surprise that must have been audible from the other side of the wall. Because what I saw first, not two feet distant, was a woman's lipstick-smeared face turned my way. Her green eyes were open but unfocussed. She had big pores and her skin shone damply beneath her jouncing curls. I recoiled so fast that I impaled myself on Loonie's front teeth. We stumbled about on the bare boards, hissing and wincing, and there was a pause in proceedings in the next room. We froze, waiting for the door to fly open. The back of my head felt punctured.

After a few very long moments, the chafing bed resumed and a man murmured and beads clacked without rhythm. I stared across at the white eye of the spyhole and when I looked back at Loonie he was laughing silently. I jerked my thumb in the direction of the door but he shook his head. At least half of me was grateful. I gathered my nerve and tiptoed back to the wall.

I pressed my eye up and saw a woman's pink rump and a man's hairy thighs thudding against it. I didn't breathe. I followed the feline curve of the woman's spine to the mass of curls on the pillow only an arm's length away from where I stood, and while I watched, Margaret Myers rose on her elbows in response to some new urgency. Her breasts and beads swung and the golden hoops of her earrings glinted. She tilted her face up and opened her eyes a moment and looked my way. There was a moment – just a flicker – of surprise but I knew she'd seen me. She seemed more interested than outraged. And gradually, with a kind of weary amusement, as the bloke pounded away behind her, she began to smile.

A hot jet ran down the leg of my jeans, and I made a stupid sound as Loonie pulled me aside to see for himself. Right then the man called out to nobody in particular, like a bloke who'd just dropped something in the street, and I didn't need to be watching to know whose voice it was. I stood clear, fully expecting Loonie to reel back out of the room at the sound of his old man right there through the wall, but he stayed where he was, lips pursed, head and palms against the tin, as though he'd seen it all before.

I'M AMAZED at how long it took me to become properly inquisitive about Sando and Eva. Anybody older might have been more than merely curious about their circumstances. For one thing, they seemed to be free agents. They lived like no other people I'd ever met. It was hardly abnormal in those years for longhairs to avoid all talk of work and money except to condemn them in proper Aquarian terms, but these two never even bothered to bring the subject up. They never spoke about making a living the way locals did; it was as if the concept never occurred to them. They thought and lived and carried themselves differently to other people. There were few townsfolk who lived as comfortably as they did yet I didn't ask why. I was a mere schoolboy. I wouldn't say that I was under anyone's spell exactly, but I did feel that there was something special about Sando and I had no interest in how people paid their bills. Of what importance are the material details of adult life when you're an adolescent? I didn't think to ask how he got what he had or even how he got to be what he was.

I put all my efforts into trying to be like him. I could take or leave his prickly wife, but I watched Sando; I hung on his every word. I was content to just be with him. There were afternoons out there with Loonie and Eva and him when we swung in hammocks while the weather piled up towards the forest from the broad sweep of the bay, as roos grazed on the grassy slope and the wind chimes stirred around us, that I had a sense I'd been singled out somehow, chosen.

Then there were those rare days, the times we returned from a session so huge, surf so terrifying as to render us incoherent. Back at the house we ate and drank and lay rocking alongside one another, laughing like stoners. It was hard to find words for the things we'd just seen and done. The events themselves resonated in your limbs. You felt shot full and the sensation burned for hours – for days, sometimes – yet you couldn't make it real for anybody else. You couldn't and you weren't sure you wanted to. But we blathered at each other from sheer excitement and you can imagine the boyish superlatives and the jargon we employed. Eva was impatient with our giggling nonsense. Yet now and then I caught her listening, especially to Sando, in a way that made me wonder about her.

Sando was good at portraying the moment you found yourself at your limit, when things multiplied around you like an hallucination. He could describe the weird, reptilian thing that happened to you: the cold, supercharged certainty which overtook your usually dithering mind, the rest of the world in a slow-motion blur around you, the tunnel vision, the surrender that confidence finally became. And when he talked about the final rush, the sense of release you felt at the end, skittering out to safety in the beautiful deep channel, Eva sometimes sank back with her eyes closed and her teeth bared, as though she understood only too well.

It's like you come pouring back into yourself, said Sando one afternoon. Like you've exploded and all the pieces of you are reassembling themselves. You're new. Shimmering. Alive.

Yes, she said. Exactly.

And I watched her, and wondered how she knew.

JUST AS I BEGAN to find some confidence, all the parameters changed. One rainy afternoon inside by the fire, Sando started talking about a break called the Nautilus. This new wave seemed so far off the scale I thought he was making it up in order to freak us out. It sounded too implausible, too deliberately mysterious. But then he brought out nautical charts and it began to look as though this spot really did exist. Sando had his own detailed sketches of the bombora and its approaches and he drew diagrams to show us the way the swell came onto the reef. He said he'd been studying it for ages, wondering if it could be surfed, certain it was a wave no other surfer had seen, let alone ridden. Despite all the charts and drawings the whole deal still sounded a bit fanciful. This wasn't a deepwater bommie like Old Smoky. The Nautilus was an oceanic lump of rock, a ship-killer barely beneath the surface. It was easy to imagine vicious whitewater in such a place, but not an evenly breaking wave of the sort we needed.

Sando watched our faces. My scepticism must have shown. From his shirt pocket he produced a solitary Polaroid. He'd obviously been saving it for last because he flipped the photo onto the table with a flourish and sat back with a smile. Neither Loonie nor I picked that shiny square up for a moment. But there it was, a thick, purple frown of water, the most impossible wave I'd ever seen.

Oh, man, you're kidding, I said. You can't surf that.

You don't reckon? he said with a grin.

I couldn't believe Sando or anyone else would even consider it. This spot was unlike anything we'd ever heard of, let alone attempted. The Nautilus was three miles out. A sharkpit. It lay seaward of a granite island – a seal colony, no less – and the wave itself broke over a huge rock which actually did look like the upright shell of a nautilus. On the charts it was marked as a navigation hazard with multiple warnings.

You launch here at the cove, he said, tapping the chart.

And you've done this? I asked.

Well, yeah, I've scoped it. Buzzed out in the dinghy a few times.

Loonie turned the Polaroid over in his hands. You took this?

Yep. Needs a lot of west in the swell.

Fuck, said Loonie. Look at this thing. How big is that?

Twenty feet, I spose.

No way!

And it's breakin square.

The reef's half outta the water, I said. It's nuts.

Yeah, said Sando with a laugh. Horrible, innit?

Aw, man, said Loonie.

The next frontier, said Sando.

I knew he'd surfed some big waves in his time. He spoke of Mexico often enough, of Indonesia and various Pacific atolls, and back here he'd taken on Old Smoky alone, paddled out time and again without a soul to watch or help. He was a pioneer; I couldn't doubt his experience or his courage. But this was something else. And I didn't know whether to feel honoured or angry that he might expect us to attempt it with him.

You think it's really possible? I asked, trying not to sound feeble. I mean, what do you really think? Honestly.

Honestly? he said. Mate, I need a shit just looking at it.

I laughed with him but Loonie turned on us.

You mean you're *scared* of it?

Sando looked a little taken aback. He shrugged. Well, a man'd be stupid not to be scared. I mean, look at this thing.

I'm scared talkin about it, I muttered.

But Loonie only scowled in disapproval.

Fear's natural, mate, said Sando. There's no shame in it.

Loonie rolled his eyes, but he stopped short of contradicting him.

Being afraid, said Sando. Proves you're alive and awake.

Whatever you reckon, said Loonie, not relishing the prospect of another of Sando's little seminars.

Animals react out of instinct, Sando continued. Like they're always on automatic. We've got plenty of that, too. But our minds complicate things, slow us down. We're always calculating the odds, measuring the consequences. But you can train your mind to live with fear and deal with the anticipation.

Aw, boys, said Eva coming into the room, where the fire smoked away untended. Now you got him going.

Every day, said Sando, making an elaborate show of ignoring her. Every day, people face down their own fears. They make calculations, bargains with God, strategic manoeuvres. That's how we first crossed oceans and learnt to fly and split the atom, how we found the nerve to give up on all the old superstitions. Sando gestured grandly at the books against the wall. That's mankind for you, he said. Our higher side. We rise to a challenge and set a course. We take a decision. You put your mind to something. Just deciding to do it gets you halfway there. Daring to try.

I cleared my throat uncertainly and he looked at me with unexpected fondness.

But that doesn't mean you don't feel fear, he continued. You can't lie about that. Denying fear, well, that's . . . unmanly.

And if you're a woman? asked Eva.

We all looked at her blankly.

I'm sure you mean *unworthy*, she said.

Sando blinked. Yeah, he murmured. Dishonourable. Dishonest. Whatever.

Husband and wife exchanged glances I couldn't interpret. I sat there trying to take all this in, only faintly consoled by the knowledge that Sando could look at that Polaroid and be afraid like me.

Of course, he said mischievously, we don't *have* to try it on. We could always go back to riding the Point when it's two foot and sunny. What d'you reckon?

He looked at us with a kind of comradely warmth that made me want to not disappoint him.

No harm lookin, I said. I guess.

Piece a piss, said Loonie.

We laughed and poked the fire and threw cushions, but underneath all the smiles and cheers I had a sick feeling. This winter I'd seen and done stuff I never could have imagined previously. Things had borne down so quickly on me that it was brain-shaking. For the past few months I'd been an outrider, a trailblazer, and the excitement and strangeness of it had changed me. There was such an intoxicating power to be had from doing things that no one else dared try. But once we started talking about the Nautilus I got the creeping sense that I'd begun something I didn't know how to finish.

Storms continued to come late that winter and into spring, but none big or westerly enough to make it worth our while giving the Nautilus a try. On the mildest October swell Sando took us out to reconnoitre the place, and it was everything he said it was. Even though it only humped up and broke intermittently while we were alongside it made me anxious to watch and I can't say I was heartbroken to be denied the chance to test myself there that year. But without swell I was overtaken by restlessness and by a boredom from which there seemed to be no relief. At school I was in freefall and at home my new lassitude set the oldies on edge. The old girl tried to broach the subject with me but I cut her dead every time. Everything around me seemed so pointless and puny. The locals in the street looked cowed and weak and ordinary. Wherever I went I felt like the last person awake in a room of sleepers. Little wonder my parents seemed so relieved when it came time for school camp.

Angelus High sent its students to stay at the old quarantine station in the bush at the harbour entrance. You could make it out a mile across the water from town but it seemed more remote than it was. I went without enthusiasm. I had a cold and I suppose in retrospect I was mildly depressed, so it was a surprise to be as struck as I was by the peculiar atmosphere of the place. The settlement itself was little more than a cluster of Victorian barracks and cottages on a patch of level ground beyond the highwater mark. The decommissioned buildings seemed hunkered down, besieged by sky and sea and landscape. The steep isthmus behind them was choked with thickets of coastal heath from which granite tors stood up at mad angles. Every human element, from the slumping rooftops to the sad little graveyard, seemed older and more forlorn than the ancient country beyond. The scrub might have been low and wizened and the stones badly weathered, but after every shower of rain they all shone; they stood up new and fresh, as though they'd only moments ago heaved themselves from the skin of the earth.

That week I slipped away at every opportunity from whichever character-building group activity we'd been wrangled into, and made my way to the cemetery or the little beach below it. From there I could gaze across to the distant wharf at Angelus whose cranes and silos looked too small to be real. It was like seeing the familiar world at a twofold remove, from another time as much as another direction, for it felt that I was in an outpost of a different era. It wasn't only the colonial buildings that gave me such a sense, but also the land they were built on. Each headstone and every gnarled grasstree spoke of a past forever present, ever-pressing, and for the first time in my life I began to feel, plain as gravity, not only was life short, but there had been so much of it.

Queenie found me feverish one afternoon in the old mortuary room. It was a derelict place full of webs and bird nests and flickering shadows and the eeriness of it distracted us from our awkwardness. We stood looking at the raised slab with its gruesome gutters and drains.

Creepy, she murmured.

Yeah, I said honking into my handkerchief. And sad. All the waiting around they did. The people stuck here. All that sitting around to be declared clean, or whatever. Just to end up on this, some of them.

I looked at her. She was sucking thoughtfully on a hank of hair and staring at the morgue slab. I'd forgotten how smart she was, how much I liked her.

You think there's ghosts? I asked offhandedly.

Probably.

You believe all that stuff? I asked, surprised.

Yes, actually. Out on the farm, she said. Down on our beach, you hear things at night.

Yeah? I sniggered. What things?

Well, people's voices. And whales. You know, singing.

Well, *that*'s not ghosts, obviously.

I don't know about that, she said. Whales are more or less extinct on this coast.

I've seen whales around.

Yeah? Alive? How many?

I shrugged. In truth I could only think of a single sighting since primary school. It was a miserable thought.

Whale ghosts.

Go ahead and laugh, she said.

I laughed. She thumped my arm. My laugh turned into a horrible cough. I was hot and clammy, but I wanted to keep her talking.

Kind of childish, don't you think?

Really? she said bridling. Maybe we'll see about that.

It transpired that I was not, after all, immune to a dare. Queenie and I spent the night in a sleeping bag on the mortuary slab. The joint we passed back and forth was damp and so stale it tasted like smouldering compost, which didn't exactly help my cough. We told each other ghoulish stories and tried to ignore the impossible chill of the channelled block beneath us. All night the corrugated-iron walls warped and flapped in the southerly and I coughed like a wild dog.

Queenie's hair crowded the single pillow we shared and despite my cold we kissed with a desperate cheerfulness. Her mouth had the vegetable taste of pot about it but it was soft and warm and I don't really know if we kissed with any purpose other than warding off the chill and whatever else lurked in the night around us. I was conscious of her limbs against mine but more aware of the cadaver slab against my back and although I felt one of her notable breasts through her woollen jumper we never quite got into the swing of things. Eventually she fell asleep to leave me suspended in a state of excruciating alertness. The hut sighed and moaned. My heart raced. I tried not to cough for fear of waking her. My skin felt too tight and I began to sweat. It was dark in that hut, black as a dog's guts, and the night got away from me.

Queenie and I were sent home from camp.

Three days later I was in hospital in Angelus with pneumonia.

I ONLY REMEMBER the dream.

I was deep. The whole sea boiled overhead. White streaks of turbulence drove down like tracer fire and rocket trails, a free-fire zone in dim and shuddering green.

And I'm plummeting, a projectile. When it comes rushing at me, black as death, the reef is shot full of holes and I slam into one, headlong.

Next, I see myself, from outside my flailing, panicked body. Headfirst. Wedged in the rock. While my lungs turn to sponge and the ocean inside me flickers with cruel light.

Drowning.

Drowning.

Fighting it.
But drowning.

There was, for a while, I'm certain, a woman at the bedside. I thought it was Eva Sanderson but it was more likely a nurse or my mother or Queenie Cookson. Whoever it was, she held my hand and spoke for a long time. But her words made no more sense than birdsong. And then she was gone.

I woke up and my parents were in the room, anxious and exhausted, still bearing on their faces the unmistakeable look of disappointment that I was to see again a few weeks later when my school report came home.

LOONIE QUIT SCHOOL. He was jack of it; he just wanted to go surfing, but his old man was having none of that and he sent him up to the mill. Loonie hated everything about it. My old man said he wouldn't last a fortnight, said Loonie wouldn't work in an iron lung, said the kid was lazy and plain dangerous as a result.

Those summer holidays I went out to Sando's nearly every day. Eva had gone to the States for a few weeks and with Loonie in the workforce I had Sando to myself. I did more than seize the opportunity; I drank it up.

On flat-calm days we dived, and if there was the slightest swell we fooled about at the Point with boards he dug out from the far recesses of the undercroft – logs from the sixties, pig-boards and weird, tear-shaped things with psychedelic sprayjobs. There were days when we just hung out, when he'd sit crosslegged on the verandah carving a piece of cypress and I'd watch in silence. That summer he taught me how to play the didjeridu, to sustain the circular breathing necessary to keep up the low, growling drone you could send down the valley from his front steps. The noise of it made the dog go bush. I liked the way it sucked energy from me and drew hard feelings up the way only a good tantrum could when I was little. I blew till I saw stars, till a puddle of drool appeared on the step below or until Sando took the thing off me.

Sometimes you didn't bother to engage Sando in conversation. When he got into a mood I left him to his own thoughts and consoled myself down in the roo paddock alone with the didj. For me, Eva's absence was a boon, but I could see how agitated it often made him. Still, most afternoons he was mellow, even expansive. When he gave you his full attention you could feel yourself quicken, like a tree finding water.

It was different having Sando to myself. With only the two of us around, the talk got away from swells and surfspots. Sometimes he launched into raves about the Spartans or Gauguin. He told me about Herman Melville in Tahiti and the death of James Cook. When I told him I'd read Jack London and tried Hemingway, he lit up. From his shelves he took down *Men and Sharks* by Hans Hass, an old hardcover edition with black and white photos.

Take it, he said, it's a present.

He told me about the dolphin meat that Javanese

fishermen had given him, how he ate it to avoid insult. He said he would eat human flesh if necessary, but hoped he'd never need to, and this was all he could think of while he ate the dolphin. We talked about the oil crisis, the prospect of nuclear annihilation. He spoke of the survivalists he'd met in Oregon and, speaking of survival, I told him of Loonie's conviction that during a wipeout he could sieve oxygen from sea-foam, suck it through his teeth to stay alive. We laughed at the loopiness of this, at Loonie's lovable denseness.

I basked in Sando's attention and treasured these brief moments of esteem. Sometimes he hugged me as I left, but more often he sent me on my way with a good-natured whack on the head.

We were in the kitchen one day, as Sando ground the spices for his special fish curry, when I saw a photo that I'd never noticed before. It hung in a sheoak frame on the dado beside the stove and its glass was speckled with oil stains. The image was a figure in a red snowsuit, a skier more or less upside down against the whiteness of a mountain. In the background were pointed trees like something from a TV Christmas.

Hey, I said. What's this?

Sando paused a moment with the mortar and pestle. The smells of coriander and cumin and turmeric were not the sort of thing that ever came from my mother's kitchen. My eyes were already itching from the vapour of crushed chillies.

That, Pikelet, is my wife.

You're shittin me.

I peered closer. Between goggles and hood there was a tuft of blonde hair. Her whole body was inverted, with her skis in the sky and her face tilted toward the ground somewhere below.

I shit you not.

Far out!

Yeah, I guess that about covers it. Pretty heavy-duty, eh.

How did she do it?

Off a jump. Big downhill run and up the ramp. Full 360.

And lands on her feet.

Well, that's the plan.

She's done it more than once, then?

Mate, she's pretty well known. It's freestyle. It's a whole other scene. They're the bad boys and girls of skiing. That's Utah in '71. She's there now.

Skiing?

Jesus, no – not with that knee. Nah, they're trying another operation.

Ah, I murmured, beginning to see.

She's been out three years now. More.

I thought about the pills, the limp, those bleak moods.

She's had other operations?

Sando nodded grimly.

Maybe this time it'll work.

Yeah, but it's a long shot.

There's no snow here, I murmured. How can she stand it?

Sando rammed the pestle against the grist of spices. I rested my chin on the benchtop and I could feel the force of his arms pulsing in the wood.

I think she prefers it here. I mean, if you couldn't surf anymore, would you want to live by the sea?

The ocean's beautiful. That'd be enough for me.

Bullshit.

No, really, I said. It'd be enough just to see it.

Believe me, you're talkin shit.

I stood up, stung by his casual certainty. It seems odd to have remembered it but in later life I had cause to recall the moment. I was in my thirties before I learnt that I too would prefer not to see what I could no longer have.

Don't sulk, he said.

I'm not, I muttered.

She's got guts, that girl.

Yes, I agreed, seeing that I'd underestimated her. Eva's photo was on the wall but none of him could be shown. I didn't get it. They had so much in common. She'd been thwarted, but as far as I could tell he'd pretty much walked away. I wondered which had required most guts.

You're not from here, I said.

Nah, Melbourne originally, he said, ignoring my peevish tone.

So, why here?

Forest. Empty beaches. Waves nobody's ridden. Came here in the sixties for a while. Had a hut up there in the trees. I was after something pure, I guess.

Pure, I said.

Yeah, I know. Is anything really that pure?

I shrugged and there was a kind of detente between us again while he ground the spices and heated the skillet and fried them slowly until the house filled with smells enough to nearly lift the place off its poles.

LOONIE WAS sacked from the mill before he could quit. In the new year his old man told him to get work in Angelus at the cannery or the meatworks, but it was a thirty-mile drive each way and without a driver's licence there was only the school bus to get him there, so he wound up washing glasses and sweeping up at the pub. He bought an old trail bike and started riding unlicensed out to Sando's along the back tracks.

Whenever he blasted up the drive in a gust of dirt and two-stroke fumes he changed the atmosphere. He came more and more often those holidays and before long my interlude with Sando was over.

Sando never said a thing about the trip to Indonesia. He certainly didn't tell me that he planned to take Loonie with him. I didn't know Loonie even had a passport or how he'd conned his old man into letting him go. Maybe he had something on him; it was the only way I could see him getting his way. I didn't know a thing. They were just, quite suddenly, gone.

The dog was left with only a pink dune of dried food and a water bowl replenished by the tap dripping at the watertank, but Sando must have known I'd keep coming out there to check on it. I sat with the dog several days in bitter silence. One afternoon I went out to find that Eva was back. She was on crutches and as pissed off as I'd ever seen her. I asked her what was going on and she called me fifty kinds of fucking bastard and told me to piss off and never come back.

IT TOOK ME a week to work up the nerve to go out and claim my board from beneath the Sandersons' house. I had hoped that Eva might be away again, but when I pushed my bike up into the clearing she was out on the verandah with the dog which barked and came skittering down to see me. She climbed awkwardly to her feet. She wore cut-off Levi's. Even from down there I could see the colour of her knee.

I just came for me twin-fin, I said, still clutching the bike.

There's coffee, she said.

Nah. I'll just get me board.

Pikelet, you don't have to take the goddamn board.

But I'm gunna.

Oh, whatever, she said, bracing herself against the verandah rail. Look, I'm sorry I chewed you out. It was a shitty thing to do.

I stood there.

Come on, have coffee. Peace.

I hesitated. The breeze had swung onshore anyway and I didn't really feel like turning around right now to pedal straight back into town. So I relented and went up.

The house was in disarray with empty plates and mugs and bottles everywhere. The sink looked like a salvage yard and everything stank of garbage and pot.

Eva's limp was so painful to see that I went ahead and got the coffee myself. I came back out onto the verandah to sit at a safe distance.

The other day, she said. I was pretty bummed out. I apologize.

I shrugged, crosslegged on the boards. I sipped the coffee without pleasure. I was still a tea man. It was quiet for a while and when I looked over she was staring out across the roo paddock. There were dark smudges around her eyes and her hair was greasy. The suture line on her knee was vivid.

How did the operation go? I asked.

No dice. I guess it was worth a shot.

I saw that photo of you. It's radical.

Well, she said too brightly. That's one for the archives now, isn't it?

I didn't know how to respond. The only things you could say were stupid.

Well, here we are, Pikelet. We're both abandoned.

He didn't tell you anything?

He left a note.

But he knew when you'd be back?

She nodded. Way to go, Sando.

So, what'll you do?

Oh, she said. I'll sit here and be pissed at him. What else am I gonna do? A few weeks he'll be back, all smiles, full of stories. Normally I wouldn't care so much, you know. But I could have done with some . . . well, some help. And you?

Me?

The lone musketeer.

I shrugged again, reminded of my humiliation.

You couldn't have gone anyway, she said. You got school and stuff. What are you, fifteen?

In a few weeks.

Your time'll come.

He coulda told me, I said. I was here every day and he coulda said.

Guru shit and bad manners are pretty much the same thing, Pikelet.

I guess, I murmured, but I didn't really know what she meant. I sat there long enough to drain the mug but I was anxious to go.

You need help with stuff? I asked, hoping that she didn't.

No, I'm fine. But thanks.

I was halfway down the stairs when she called out that some fresh fish would be nice, if I ever went spearing. I said I'd keep it in mind, but I had no plans to be back.

The dog followed me all the way out to the road and stood in the drive while I pedalled off. It looked at me dolefully, as though I'd abandoned it to its grim mistress.

FOR WEEKS I smarted with a feeling of having been overlooked – forsaken, unchosen – and the shock of it was all the greater because of how much I'd lately come to imagine an advantage over Loonie. I thought Sando and I had a special bond, a kind of intellectual interest, something Loonie, for all his animal energy, couldn't match. And now I felt like such an idiot.

I left for school and returned again sullen enough to irritate the old folks. At night in bed I conjured up the knowing smile Margaret Myers shot me that day in the pub and I jerked off morosely while the wind poured through the trees and the house creaked on its stumps.

Queenie took up with the captain of the school football team. He had a car, and sideburns like Peter Fonda.

At day's end I slumped in the bus, overcome by ordinariness.

Some evenings I swam in the river where the primary-schoolers bombed off the old plank. Once or twice I clung to roots on the bottom and deluded myself into thinking that up on the surface the little kids' wonder was turning to panic, but I doubt anybody even remembered I was there.

The next Saturday, I surfed the Point with the Angelus crew who seemed a little leery of me, but Sunday was hot and the sea mirror-flat so I spent the hours spearing fish behind the headland. I filled a hessian sack with queenies, harlequins and boarfish, and it was some business humping it back with my gear to the bike. Well before I drew up at the Sandersons' drive I knew I had no hope of riding the full bag home. I didn't want to go up there. But I couldn't bring myself to start slinging good fish into the bush.

Eva seemed unusually pleased to see me. While I filleted the snapper in the shade of the killing tree she came downstairs with Cokes. Her leg was strapped and her limp was still severe, but she seemed more sanguine than I'd seen her for a while. I cut the red meat from the fish's shoulder and gave it to the dog. Eva sat in the shade and passed me a glass.

I had Loonie's father out here today, she said. Man, is he pissed.

Pissed? I asked. Like, drunk?

No, pissed as in pissed off. He expected Loonie back Friday.

Friday? Is that when Sando said he'd be back?

Oh, who knows. When he's away the schedule's kind of open-ended. Seems the old man wasn't so happy about Loonie going anyways. Man, you can see the son in the father, huh?

I shrugged.

They have a way of looking at you, she said. Like you're some kind of . . . abomination.

Because you're American?

Naw, because I'm a fee-male.

Oh.

He's on his own, huh?

Um, I dunno, I said, tempted to broach the subject of Margaret Myers.

Guess I should feel sorry for him. But I don't.

I figured that my knowledge of the publican and Margaret Myers might include some awkward details, so I left it alone.

Do you miss it? I asked.

She looked at me. Miss what, exactly?

The snow. Sando told me about freestyling.

Of course I miss it, she said. Kinda dumbass question is that?

She drank her Coke and banged the glass down on the plank beside me. I trimmed the fillets and set them on the plate for her, determined to clean up and leave as quickly as I could.

How can you get em back on the farm once they've seen Paree.

Sorry? I wiped blood and scales from the knife.

Once you've had a taste of something different, something kind of *out there,* then it's hard to give it up. Gets its hooks in you. Afterwards nothing else can make you feel the same.

I nodded, understanding finally.

I guess I miss the buzz, she said. Boy, we did some scary shit up on the mountain. But, you know how it is, time wounds all heels. Your moment arrives and just slips away. Kinda cruel, huh.

Maybe it'll just get better on its own.

Yeah, and maybe Santy Clause is a Jew.

Stung, I slunk across to the watertank to wash my hands. The dog licked the salt off my legs.

I've never seen snow, I said.

White, she said. And cold. Thanks for the fish.

She had a way of making you feel small and stupid, even when she was in a good mood. I remembered again how little I liked her.

The week before Sando and Loonie finally returned, brown and shiny-eyed from Bali, I went back to see Eva. I had no fish; I was bored and lonely, fed up and spoiling for a blue. I was ready to tell that fancy Yank what I thought of her.

Months previous, Sando had rigged an exercise contraption on the verandah, an arrangement of weights and pulleys for Eva to use to strengthen her leg. I'd never known her to use it, but when I mounted the stairs she was cranking the thing without let-up. She saw me but didn't stop. She was mottled, slick with sweat, so fierce in her pain that it took me aback. I felt a chill of apprehension. But I stood there, trapped by her gaze, all the wind gone from my sails. I felt I'd stumbled into something private. It was awkward but I didn't dare leave. She went on a full five minutes before pitching back, totally spent.

Throw me a towel!

I was affronted but hapless.

Gimme. The fucking. Towel!

I saw that a towel hung from the verandah rail beside me. I pulled it free and bunched it a moment, then hurled it with more force than was necessary. She caught the thing and buried her face in it. Her chest heaved so sharply I wondered if she was weeping, but I was more curious than sympathetic.

A breeze stirred the chimes around us. I didn't know why I stood there; it was my chance to bolt.

Oh, she said at last, wiping her boiled-looking face. I need a shower.

I'm off, then.

Stay, she said. I'll make coffee.

I don't bloody drink coffee.

Okay, Coke. We'll talk. Hey, I haven't fed the dog. The sack's still in the car. D'you mind?

I went down into the yard with the dog and found the big pack of dog food and poured out a dish on the ground. When she came out onto the verandah, Eva's hair was slicked back and her eyes were bright. Barefoot, in a sleeveless cotton dress, she seemed calm. It was as though the storm of pain had passed. She flopped into a hammock and swung there.

I'm hungry, she said. Can you cook?

I shook my head.

Didn't think so. C'mon, let's make burgers. I got supplies this morning.

For an hour or so she bossed me about in the kitchen and eventually we ate in silence off the benchtop. We sat on the stools Sando had made from bushwood. It was odd, this making-do. Neither of us was the other's first preference for company. We were stuck with each other.

Once she'd eaten, Eva became unusually talkative. We went back out onto the verandah and slouched into hammocks and she told me about growing up in Salt Lake City, about Mormons and mountains and her dead mother. Wryly, she explained the business of college scholarships and the startling advent of the angel Moroni. She told me stuff about new religion and new money that I couldn't quite grasp, and the longer she went on, the stranger America seemed to be.

On TV Americans were so soft and sentimental, all happy-go-lucky and forever safely at home. But the way Eva told it, her countrymen were restless, nomadic, clogging freeways and airports in their fevered search for action. She said they were driven by ambition in a way that no Australian could possibly understand. They wanted fresh angles, better service, perfect mobility. I tried to picture what she meant. She made her own people sound vicious. Yet God was in everything – all the talk, all the music, even on their money. Ambition, she said. Aspiration and mortal anxiety.

It was hard to negotiate the tangled crosscurrents of pride and disgust in Eva's rambling account, but it gave me plenty to think about. Here in Sawyer people seemed settled – rusted on, in fact. They liked to be ordinary. They were uncomfortable with ambition and avoided any kind of unpredictability or risk. There was a certain muted grandeur in our landscape but it seemed that power and destiny did not adhere to bare plains and dank forest. There were no mighty canyons and mile-wide rivers here. Without soaring peaks and snow, angels seemed unlikely and God barely possible.

I don't know how long I lay there in my hammock, ruminating on all this, before I realized that Eva had long since stopped talking. A light drizzle began to fall. Hauling up onto an elbow I saw she was asleep. Her hair had dried in a snarl beneath her. The tightness was gone from her face. Now and then her eyelids twitched and fluttered. She gave out a light, intermittent snore. Where her dress rode up her legs were pale.

It seemed wrong to stare at Eva like this, but I'd never been able to properly look at her before. I'd only ever known her in glances, from glimpses snatched in moments when I thought I was safe from her scalding glare. I eased myself out of the hammock and crept up beside her. She smelled of shampoo and fried onions. I studied the scars on her misshapen knee. The freshest suture line was fat and angry, a centipede imbedded in her flesh; it overlaid its predecessors, a silvery nest of them like a fossil record. There was stubble on her shins. For a moment, while she slept, she had gooseflesh on her arms.

I had the sudden and perilous urge to touch her. I wanted to feel her ruined knee and I didn't know why. I reached out.

Don't hurt me, she said.

I flinched and stepped back, knocking a chair against the wall. Eva sat up, confused and awake.

What is it?

I shook my head. I gotta go.

LOONIE SHOWED UP one night while I was failing to do my homework. I could see the mixed look on my mother's face as she ushered him into my room. She was fond of Loonie but her old wariness was back. She pulled at his strawy hair a moment and squeezed his shoulder as she left.

Did I miss anythin? he asked. No swell?

I shook my head.

Far out, he said abstractedly. He sat on my bed and flipped through the social studies book lying there.

So, I said. How was it?

He put the book down and pursed his lips. Fuckin unbelievable.

When'd you get back?

Last night. The old man's gone spastic. Hey, cop this.

Loonie pushed up the sleeve of his windcheater to reveal a long, pulpy wound.

Uluwatu, he murmured. It's insane.

What happened?

Just the reef. That coral rips the shit outta you.

For half an hour he told me stories of lonely waves and temples and paddies, of monkeys and offerings and incense smoke; how Sando and he ate turtle meat and coconuts and rode out to reefs on outrigger canoes. I felt a stubborn refusal to be impressed. The more Loonie talked, the less I responded. I could see it puzzling him. He reached for bigger stories, wilder moments, to little avail.

I brought you this, he said, setting a tamped wad of foil on the desk beside me. It was no bigger than a .22 rifle cartridge.

What is it?

Hash, mate.

Jesus, I murmured.

Well, don't have a baby.

I heard the old girl coming before she had time to open the door. The little foil bullet fell into the drawer and Loonie met her on his way out.

Things were different after Sando and Loonie returned from the islands. If there was a swell big enough they might come by on weekends. We all surfed Barney's several times in late summer and even saw its terrible namesake, but for the most part I found myself on the outside of whatever it was the other two had going. Loonie's time in Indonesia had granted him a new kind of seniority. He'd seen animal sacrifices and shamans and walked on black, volcanic beaches. He'd climbed down the legendary cave at Uluwatu and paddled out, bombed to the gills on hash. Yet here I was, still a schoolboy.

Sando was distant now, preoccupied. He seemed suddenly closed off from me. I began to sense that there were secrets between him and Loonie, things they kept from me with grins and furtive glances. When we surfed they gave off a physical arrogance that might simply have been confidence born of experience, but I felt cowed by it. Now I understood the looks that the Angelus crew shot me. It was how they saw us – the little Brahman circle.

I didn't see much of Eva, but when I did she was drawn and unhappy. A new current of antagonism flashed between her and Sando. She did her best to act as though Loonie didn't exist.

A MONSTER STORM showed up before autumn even arrived. On the forecast maps it looked like a tumour on the sea between us and the southern iceshelf. The moment he saw it Sando began planning our attempt on the Nautilus. On the Saturday and Sunday before the front arrived the swell in its path hadn't yet gathered momentum. We'd have to wait for the passage of the storm and catch the swell in its wake. Which meant I'd have to wag school if I wanted to make the trip.

Before the wind had even stirred the trees I knew I wasn't ready for the Nautilus. On the night the storm descended I lay in bed feeling the roof quake, wondering how I could plausibly avoid the whole endeavour. For two days black squalls ripped in from the sea and rain strafed the roads and paddocks and forest. On the morning of the third day, while it was still full dark and spookily still, I woke to a rumble that caused the house stumps to vibrate. If you didn't know any better you'd have thought a convoy of tanks was advancing up our drive and into the forest behind us. It was a low, grinding noise, a menacing pulse that didn't let up for a moment. I got out of bed feeling queasy. I packed a towel and wetsuit into my school bag, ate a couple of cold sausages from the fridge and waited for the dawn.

I got to the bus stop outside the butcher's about a half-hour early, figuring that if Sando didn't come then I'd just go ahead and take the bus to school. This morning school was an attractive option. But a few moments later, Loonie showed up blowing steamy breath on his hands, and before we'd even begun to speak the VW with its trailer and dinghy pulled in.

It was quite a drive west through the forest and then out along fishing tracks to the lonely little beach inshore of the island. All the way over Sando and Loonie psyched themselves up, each feeding off the other's nervous energy, while I sat pressed to the window, silent and afraid.

For any soul with a taste for excitement the mere business of launching Sando's dinghy should have been thrill enough for one day. The cove was a maelstrom with waves breaking end to end across it and the shorebreak heaved down with such force it sent broken kelp and shell-slurry into the air. We hauled the boat bow-out, timed our launch between waves and got the motor going, but we almost came to grief as a rogue set rumbled into the bay. By that stage there was nowhere for us to go but out, so we headed straight at those looming broken lines of foam with the throttle wide open in the hope they'd green up again before we reached them. We grabbed any handhold we could find. I felt the wind rip at my hair. And somehow we made it. As we slammed up each in turn we were airborne and the prop bawled before we landed again with a shattering thump. Loonie hooted like a rodeo rider; he'd have flapped a hat had there been one available. We found safe water, but it wasn't a good start to my day at the Nautilus. I rode the rest of the way rattled and sweating in my wetsuit. The granite island and its clump of seals were awash. The sea beyond was black and agitated.

We pulled up near the break during a lull and stood off in deep water to landward just to wait and watch before anchoring. There wasn't much to see at first except a scum of spent foam on the surface. Ocean and air seemed hyper-oxygenated; everything fizzed and spritzed as if long after the passage of previous waves there was energy yet to be dissipated. The land behind us was partly obscured by the island and a low, cold vapour the morning sun failed to penetrate. Nothing shone. The sea looked bottomless.

Only when the first new wave arrived did I see what really lay before us. It came in at an angle, just a hard ridge of swell, but within a few seconds, as it found shallow water, it became so engorged as to triple in volume. And there at its feet lay the great hump of rock that gave the place its name. The mass of water foundered a moment, distorting as it hit the submerged obstacle. The wave reared as though climbing the obstruction and then sagged drastically at each end before the yawning lip pitched forward with a sound that made me want to shit.

Fifteen foot, said Loonie.

Yeah, Sando replied. And it's breakin in three feet of water.

In fact there were times when the wave broke over no water at all. Every set brought a smoker that sucked everything before it as it bore down, dragging so much water off the rock as it gathered itself that when it finally keeled over to break the granite dome sat free and clear before it. At these moments the trough of the wave actually sank below sea level. It was a sight I had never imagined, the most dangerous wave I'd ever seen.

We watched a couple of sets and then anchored up at a distance before Sando dived in and led us out. All three boards were Brewers – long, heavy Hawaiian-style guns. They were the same equipment we used at Old Smoky and Sando kept saying how good and solid they felt. He kept up the usual inspirational patter, but I was sullen with fright. Every time he tried to make eye contact I looked away, paddling without conviction until he drew ahead with Loonie at his elbow going stroke for stroke.

They sat up together outside the boil while I hung well back in deep water. Behind us the dinghy yanked at its rope, disappearing between swells. Sets came and went but everything passed by unridden. The waves were big but even at half the size I thought they'd be too sudden, way too steep, and the shallow rock beneath made them unthinkable. True, it was an awesome sight but the whole deal only broke for fifty yards or so; it was hardly worth the risk. I watched Sando and Loonie out there, right in the zone, letting wave after wave go by as if they'd come to the same conclusion despite themselves.

Then a wide one swung through and Sando went for it.

I saw the distant flash of his teeth as he fought to get up sufficient speed. A moment later it was vertical and so was he. As he got to his feet it was obvious the board was too long for the contour of the wave; he was perilously slow to turn. The wave hurled itself inside out. Sando staggered a moment, almost falling out of the face altogether. But he kept his feet and cranked the Brewer around with a strength I knew was beyond me. The fin bit. He surged forward as the wave began to lurch and dilate, reef fuming and gurgling below. The lip pitched over him. He was gone a moment, like a bone in the thing's throat. And then a squall of spume belched him free and it was over. He skidded out into the deep, dead water ahead of me and let the board flutter away.

I dug my way across, retrieved the Brewer and steered it back to where he lay with his knees up and his head back.

Jesus, he murmured. Oh Jesus.

I sat beside him, holding the big board between us. He slowly got his breath back but he was wild-eyed.

When you go, he said, go wide and early.

Don't think so, I muttered.

He took his board, checked the fin and got on.

You get half a second, that's all; it's brutal.

I shook my head.

C'mon, Pikelet. You know what's what.

That's why I'm stayin right here.

I didn't bring you here to watch, did I?

I said nothing.

It'll put some fizz in your jizz.

I felt plenty scared but not panicked; this time I knew what I was doing.

Shit, he said. I thought I brought surfers with me. Men above the ordinary.

I shrugged.

Pikelet, mate. We came to play.

He was grinning as he said it but I felt a sort of menace from him then. I didn't give a damn. My mind was made up. He wheeled around in disgust and I watched him paddle back out to where Loonie scratched uncertainly between looming peaks.

When Sando sat up beside him Loonie straightened a little, as if fortified by his presence, and only a few moments later he took the place on. But the wave he set himself for was a shocker. It was wedge-shaped and rearing – butt-ugly – even before he got going. As he leapt to his feet you could see what was about to happen. Yet the next few awful seconds earned Loonie honour in defeat. The wave stood, hesitated, and then foundered with Loonie right at the crest. He'd assumed his desperate crouch, pointed the board to the sanctuary of the channel, but he was going nowhere but down. The wave subsided beneath him, sucked him with it. Great overpiling gouts of whitewater leapt off the reef and the most I could see of Loonie was a threshing arm. Half his board fluttered thirty feet in the air. For a horrible moment the granite dome of the reef was completely bare. Then all that broken water mobbed across the rock, driving Loonie before it, boiling off into the deep ahead of me while I sat there, rigid. The air was hissing, the sea bubbled underfoot, and I knew Loonie was down there somewhere in the white slick having the shit kicked out of him, but I didn't move until I heard Sando's furious yell.

It was whiteout down there. The water was mad with current. It was like diving blind into a crowd, and I groped, hauled off at angles until I saw the bluish contours of the seabed below. I dived again and got nowhere. I hit the surface, saw Sando – still yards off – hauling himself my way, and then I heard Loonie's gasp and turned to see his upraised arm. He was twenty yards behind me, even closer to the boat than I was.

When I got there I swept him up onto my board and listened to him puke and breathe and puke some more. The back was out of his wetsuit and there was skin off his shoulders. His nose bled, his legs trembled, but by the time Sando reached us he was laughing.

I was gutted by that day at the Nautilus. A small, cool part of me knew it was stupid to have been out there trying to surf a wave so unlikely, so dangerous, so perverse. What would success there really mean – perhaps three or four or even five seconds of upright travel on a wave as ugly as a civic monument? You could barely call such a mad scramble *surfing*. Surely there were better and bigger waves to ride than that deformity. Yet nothing could assuage the lingering sense of failure I was left with.

The others didn't mention it. All three of us celebrated Loonie's moment of defiance, but the gap had widened between them and me. He who hesitates, as I discovered, is lost indeed. I began to feel that their delicacy on the subject of my cowardice only made things worse. At first I was grateful, but soon I wished they'd just come out and call me yellow and have done with it. I hated the coy looks, the sudden gaps in conversation that reinforced my sense of relegation.

Loonie and Sando planned new assaults on the Nautilus using shorter boards – two only – shaped for the purpose. We never broached the subject of whether I'd accompany them. God knows, I should have been relieved, but I was inconsolable. I knew any reasonable person would have done what I did out there that day. Which was exactly the problem: I was, after all, ordinary.

FOR A FEW YEARS as a teenager in Sawyer, it seemed I had control of my own life. I didn't understand everything going on around me, but for a brief period I had something special that afforded me a private sense of power. It let me feel bigger, more vivid than I'd been before. Although I was no leper at school I never really made much social headway. Classmates thought I was standoffish. Some said I was up myself and none of it worried me because for a couple of years I went home from Angelus every day harbouring a consoling secret. I did stuff other people couldn't do, things they wouldn't dream of. I belonged to an exclusive club, drove around with a full-grown man and a mate who spooked people. Even among surfers we had enigmatic status. When we deigned to paddle out at the Point you could sense everyone else's deferral. Older, vaguely threatening blokes like Slipper were grudgingly respectful, especially in the presence of our mentor. Whenever some mouthy grommet started quizzing us about Sando he would be quickly silenced by one of the older crew. They knew by now that he'd surfed Old Smoky on his own for years. He was in his own league; we'd all sensed it instinctively. Sando radiated gravitas. And I got used to the power of association.

But when Sando first took Loonie to the islands, he left me behind in more than a literal sense. Somehow I stayed behind. I lost confidence in my place and value. It's possible some of my sense of relegation was imaginary or the result of shame, but I was convinced that Sando no longer took me seriously, that Loonie didn't regard me as an equal anymore, and the rich feeling of being in charge of myself evaporated. For the first time in my life I was not so much solitary as plain lonely.

Not long after Easter, in the first week of the term break, an unexpectedly vicious cold front burst upon the coast. Wind tore trees from the ground and blew roofing iron deep into the forest, and when the storm was spent it left the kind of booming swell that kept me awake half the night with that old mix of excitement and apprehension.

I waited for the sound of the Volkswagen but Loonie and Sando didn't show. About eight o'clock, while the oldies were off in town, I got on my bike and rode out to the coast.

From way across the estuary curtains of spray were visible at the rivermouth.

At Sando's the boat and the Kombi were gone; they'd opted for the Nautilus. I could hardly blame them for blowing me off but it provoked something in me. The dog didn't bark as it trotted down and I was relieved because I wanted to get in and go without waking Eva. It followed me into the undercroft where I pulled out the big yellow Brewer I'd disgraced myself with a few weeks before. I waxed the board with a block from the Milo tin on the bench and walked back down the drive with it. There was no way I could ride a bike and carry that great spear of a thing, so I hoofed it out to the headland and by the time I'd hiked across the ridges to the clifftop overlooking Old Smoky, the sun had broken through and I was clammy with sweat. My right arm felt wrenched from carrying the board so far. I did some stretches while the bombora cracked and flared out on the sunlit sea.

I don't know why I paddled out there on my own. I was hurt and angry. And I suppose I felt there was a point to prove. I knew Old Smoky had been surfed solo before. But not by a fifteen-year-old. At this distance it seems like an act of desperation – or worse – a lunge toward oblivion. Even now I can barely believe I did it.

Before I got halfway out to the bommie, it dawned on me that Old Smoky was breaking much bigger than I'd seen it before. Between long, deceptive lulls, waves angled in to stand up twenty feet and more, and by the time I got close I knew I'd seriously underestimated the size of the swell. At this scale, it was a wonder the wave still broke cleanly.

I hummed. I spoke aloud to myself. I manoeuvred into position over the reef and checked and rechecked my bearings as I'd been taught. The offshore breeze fanned up a steady chop and beneath the surface the water was busy.

I was right on the lump when a new set of swells wheeled in from the south-west. They quickened as they got a footing on the shoal and soon I was labouring uphill time and again to get beyond them. Each seemed bigger than the one before and every time I squeaked over and tumbled down into the trough behind, I was blinded by spray. In all that stinging white confusion I failed to see the third wave until it was too late. It was already seething, beginning to break, and by then it was a matter of riding it or wearing it, so I turned and went.

All the way down the big board chattered against the surface chop; I could hear the giggle and natter of it over the thunder behind me. When the wave drew itself up to its full height, walling a hundred yards ahead as I swept down, it seemed to create its own weather. There was suddenly no wind at all and the lower I got, the smoother the water became. The whole rolling edifice glistened. For a moment – just a brief second of enchantment – I felt weightless, a moth riding light. Then I leant into a turn and accelerated and the force of it slammed through my knees, thighs, bladder, and I came lofting back to the crest to feel the land breeze in my face and catch a smudge of cliffs before sailing down the line again. With each turn, each stalling fade, I grew in confidence. By the wave's last section I was styling. I scudded out into the channel, so addled by joy I had to sit a while to clear my head.

I felt fabulous, completely charged. I was not a coward or a kook. I knew what I was doing and it wasn't within a bull's roar of being ordinary.

In retrospect I know I should have sat there glorying a bit longer, given myself a full soak of fuckoff vindication until I got over myself and had a laugh at my own expense. Then I could have gone about the business of putting the act back together, gathering my thoughts, returning to some method. But I was so amped and eager I just wheeled about, paddled back into the impact zone and picked off the first wave of the next set. Compounding the first mistake with a second, I rushed at the thing instead of letting it come to me, and so I never quite got into position and had to scramble to get momentum. As the wave peaked I dug hard and felt myself pitch forward, teetering at the crest, surging for a few yards only to feel the wave forge ahead without me.

I knew before I even sat up and looked back over my shoulder that I was in strife. I'd left myself bang in the path of the following wave – which was bigger again and already breaking. In the seconds left I sprinted for the channel but I knew I'd never get there. I pumped myself full of air, hyperventilating hurriedly, and at the last possible moment, as the crashing white wall came down, I stood on my stationary board and speared deep as I could get. I kicked hard but in an instant the white-water smashed in, blasting me sideways, hurling me down. I saw hazy outlines of rocks. Kelp flew by. My ears hurt badly but I couldn't equalize, and then I was pitching end over end across the bottom, glancing off things hard and soft until slowly, like a storm petering out, the water slackened around me and I floundered up toward the light.

I broke the surface in a drift of foamscum and barely got a breath before another tower of whitewater crashed over, and this second hold-down was worse. I'd started with less air and got worked harder, longer. When I kicked up it was into the path of a third wave, and then there was a fourth. Each breath was more hurried, each dive just a bit shallower than the last. I got so strung out and disoriented I ploughed headfirst into the seabed, thinking I was headed for the surface. Burns and tingles shot up my legs. I saw light where there was no light. My gut began to twitch. Things went narrow – it was like looking out through a letter-box – and out there, at the other end of the slot, the white world was trying to kill me.

But when the sea let go and the water cleared I clawed up into the sky. For a moment, at the surface, it seemed my throat was jammed shut. I couldn't make myself breathe. And then wretching spasms overtook me and bile and seawater poured out and the air burnt down sharp as any regret.

There was no sign of the yellow Brewer. Once I got control of myself I saw I'd been bulldozed, mostly underwater, for four hundred yards. The only way home from here was to swim.

It took me an hour or so to reach the cliffs and maybe another thirty minutes to make it up them. I got seasick treading water in the moiling backwash. And at the end, when I wondered if I had the strength to hold out much longer, I came in on the back of a huge, blunt roller which set me down on a ledge from which I could crawl, very slowly, to safety.

When I got back to Sando's I tried to keep clear of the house but I so badly needed a drink. Eva caught me gulping from the rain-water tank.

Pikelet?

I'm just goin, I croaked.

Saw your bike. Where you been?

I shrugged, but I was standing there in my wetsuit and my knees were crusted with blood.

I gotta go.

Come up here.

No, I'm off.

You heard me. Jesus, look at you. Get up here.

I stumped slowly up the stairs and onto the verandah.

You went out there on your own, didn't you?

I lost his Brewer. The yellow one.

You mean you *swam in*? Let me look at you.

I'm just thirsty. I feel bad about the board.

Oh, forget the goddamn board. Sit down and I'll get you something.

The moment I sat I felt overcome with fatigue. I must have dozed because when I looked up she was there already with a Coke and a plate of sandwiches. I ate and drank greedily while she watched.

You take him too seriously, she said at last.

Who?

You know who. I'll get something for those gashes. Stay here.

But I didn't stay there for fear of falling asleep again. I followed her into the house and propped myself up against the kitchen bench while she rummaged in a cupboard.

Sit down before you fall over, she said. You'll have to wait until they get back. You're in no shape to ride home.

I can ride, I said. I had no intention of still being there when Sando got back.

Will you just sit the fuck down.

I did as I was told. Suddenly I was close to tears.

He tell you they're heading to Java?

I shook my head, unable to speak.

It's just not funny anymore. I don't know if I'll be here when he gets back.

She wielded a fistful of cotton balls and a bottle of something nasty-yellow. I blinked.

Jesus, why'm I telling *you* this?

I could only shrug.

Hey, she murmured. Pikelet, you won't say anything, will you?

No.

She looked at me appraisingly, and when she unscrewed the bottle and poured antiseptic into the cotton her hands shook. She took me by the chin and tilted my head up to press the scouring stuff cold to my brow and I tried not to wince.

She put the bottle down and fingered through my hair a moment to find the divot in my scalp. I looked at the pale hairs around her navel where her windcheater rode up.

You'll live.

She was a foot away. She smelled of butter and cucumber and coffee and antiseptic. I wanted to press my face into that belly, to hold her by the hips, but I sat there until she stepped away. And then I got up and left; I didn't care what she said. I rode home slow and sore and raddled.

That evening, while the day's warmth leached into the forest shadow, I sat against an ancient karri tree to smoke the hash Loonie brought me. At dinner I ate my chops with elaborate caution, anxious at every quizzical glance. I felt transparent, light, uncomfortable. In the night I dreamt my drowning dream. There I was again, head jammed tight in the reef, and when I woke, touching the tender parts of my brow and scalp, it took a while to believe it had only been a dream.

You've been in a fight, said the old man at breakfast.

No, I said.

Look at you. You may's well tell me.

It's nothin, Dad.

Face like a bird-pecked apple, said the old girl.

What the hell d'you get up to? he said with more dismay than anger in his voice.

I fell on the rocks, I murmured.

Out the coast?

Yeah.

How many times have I told you —

Tell me about Snowy Muir, I said.

The old man snatched up his hat and his workbag.

You never told me the story, I said more gently.

Some of us have got work to do, he said. He kissed my mother, stuffed his hat on his balding head and made for the door.

LOONIE WAS outside the butcher shop in the drizzle when I got off the school bus. He had the fading remains of a black eye and his lip was split in a whole new way. I didn't need to ask. I knew it'd be his old man. Loonie had told him he was going away again.

You went out to Old Smoky on your own, he said.

I shrugged and hoisted the bag onto my shoulder.

Fuck, he murmured. He's pissed off about the board.

You broke two already yourself, I said. Anyway, who told you?

She did.

Eva? She told *you*?

Nah. I heard em bluin and bitchin. She sorta blurted it out. Said you went on your own. And the board's gone, isn't it?

Swam in.

Fuck.

Did you do Nautilus? I asked despite myself.

Man, it was bullshit. I got three. Barrelled every time.

Him?

He got one. But he's fuckin scared of it.

I blinked at this.

Old, said Loonie.

There was something pitiless in his smirk.

And he's takin you to Java, I said.

Who told you that?

Eva, I said with a hot flash of satisfaction.

He grunted and rolled himself a fag and I realized that we were no longer friends. At the intersection, where the pub loomed over the servo across the road, we each veered in our own direction without even saying goodbye. Neither of us could have known that we'd never meet again.

SANDO PULLED UP at the school oval one lunch hour while I was kicking a football with a bunch of kids I barely knew. It was the old sound of the VW that caught my attention. I saw him parked over behind the goalposts but didn't go across right away. By the time I relented there were only a few minutes before the bell went again.

He sprawled over the wheel like a bus driver. He had a denim jacket on, and a silk shirt of some kind of shimmering green, and his hair and beard and earrings shone in the early winter light. He raised his eyebrows as if surprised to see me. I stood there in my grisly brown uniform.

You're off, then.

Yeah, he said. Tomorrow.

I nodded and looked out across the rooftops of Angelus.

Thought you might come out for a send-off. We don't see you much anymore.

I glanced back at the kids punting the pill from pack to pack.

I can't, I said. The oldies wouldn't let me.

He nodded, scratched in his beard pensively.

Hey, someone found the yellow Brewer.

Really?

Tuna fisherman. Twenty-five mile out, he reckons.

He give it back?

Sando nodded. I kept the flood of relief and amazement to myself.

Eva said you looked pretty shabby when you got back.

It was big, I said. It's a tough swim.

Gutsy effort, he said. All of it. You should know that. It's right up there.

I shrugged.

No, I mean it, Pikelet. Hats off.

I shoved my hands into my pockets in the effort to resist his approval. There was a long, potent silence between us and then the school bell went. Sando cranked up the Kombi.

Seeya, then.

Okay, I said.

When I got home the yellow Brewer was standing up against the shed with its big black fin jutting out like a crow's wing.

He said you could have it, said my mother. The gypsy-looking fella. Said you'd earned it.

I nodded as I took it down and held it under my arm. It was a beautiful thing, made by a master.

What job were you doing? she asked.

The usual, I said. Choppin wood.

Ah, she said. And I could see how badly she needed to believe it.

A WEEK OR SO after Sando and Loonie left, I rode out to the coast in a funk. I was sick of the hangdog looks the oldies were giving me. I was bored and angry – as lonely as I'd been in my life.

The sea was its usual wintry mess, the beach empty. I didn't particularly want to see Eva. I half thought she'd be gone anyway, as threatened. There was nowhere else to go.

The Volkswagen was parked under cover. The dog bounced out to meet me as if it'd been starved of company. I squatted with it for a while, ruffling its ears, basking in its adoration. Maybe it's an old man's delusion but it occurs to me now that a dog like that might have been good for me as a teenager. As I hunkered there, scratching the dog's belly, I thought about taking it for a ramble up the paddocks into the forest, to let it dart in and out of the shadows chasing rabbits while I talked a load of shit to it and got things off my chest. And I wish I had. Instead I went on up the stairs.

Eva was in the livingroom behind the glass doors. I saw her watching me from where she sprawled on the sofa. She wasn't quite right, the way she lay with her mouth slightly ajar and her hair mussed. I stood in the cold until she motioned me in.

The house smelled of woodsmoke and fried bacon and hash. Supertramp played quietly on the stereo. Eva wore old track pants and a Yale tee-shirt with bright yellow stains on it.

Gonna rain again, she murmured.

Yeah, I said. Wait five minutes. New weather.

I been waiting five minutes all my life. Only thing changes *is* the freakin weather.

I had nothing to say to this. I was already getting set to leave.

Pikelet, she said. Where can you get ground turkey in this country?

Ground what?

Turkey mincemeat. Where do I go?

Hell, I muttered. How would I know?

She snorted as if I was a simpleton, but I'd never heard of people eating minced turkey. At our place we didn't even have turkey at Christmas – it was no better than roadkill.

Sit down a minute.

It's hot in here, I said, perching beside her on the couch.

So take off your coat.

I saw that she had hell's own blaze going in the hearth.

Come to that, take off your shirt.

What?

You heard me.

You're stoned, I said.

But you want to. You'll do it anyway.

I thought about what might happen. It was like being in a shed with Loonie and something sharp. My body thrilled to the danger in the room.

I began to get up. She grabbed a fistful of my tee-shirt and twisted it with a kind of sneer and I looked at her in confused anger before I shrugged her off. I shucked the shirt anyway and held it gormlessly in my lap. The sneer melted from her face then and she looked almost sad. She touched my belly with her knuckles. There was a kind of disinterest in the way she held them against me and ran them slowly up my chest. I was unprepared for the painful force with which she grabbed my nipple, but she kissed my neck so softly my whole scalp flushed with something like gooseflesh. She kissed me on the neck again and again, unbuckling my Levi's all the while, and when I came she laughed in my ear like someone who'd won a bet.

I followed her to the loft. She kicked off her clothes, fell onto the unmade bed and smiled at me with something like tenderness. I felt a great force rising behind me, pressing me on.

Pikelet, you don't have to.

Oh, I said with false brightness. Maybe I do. Maybe I will.

Okay, she said. Now where did I leave those instructions?

I shoved off my damp jeans and clambered onto the bed and kissed her inexpertly. Eva's hair was unwashed and her mouth tasted of hash and coffee. Her fingers were stained with turmeric. She smelled of sweat and fried coconut. She was heavier than me, stronger. Her back was broad and her arms solid. There was nothing thin and girly about her. She did not close her eyes. She did not wait for me to figure things out for myself.

In the afternoon, when we'd eaten her curry and smoked the rest of her hash, she saw me standing in the living-room, looking at all their stuff. I was stoned and emboldened. I felt older, pleased with myself, and for some reason I was noticing for the first time just how new and choice everything was. One day, I told myself, I want gear like this.

What? she said, cutting up a grapefruit.

Nothin.

Bullshit. You're thinking where does all the money come from.

No. Not really.

Jesus, Pikelet. You're like a book.

I shrugged. She was wrong but I didn't want to look any more stupid than I was.

It's a trust account thing. My father's money.

For Sando too?

She smiled. Yeah, him too. But they don't get along, my dad and him.

But that's how he can —

Surf and travel, yeah. How I could be a skier. Sure.

I was bombed. I didn't really know what a trust fund was but I felt the distance it put between us; it was bigger than the gap in our nationalities, even our ages. Money just showing up in a bank account. Without work. I said nothing but Eva must have seen it in my face.

The big, bad world, Pikelet. It is what it is.

Wow.

Guess it's not fair, but so what.

I spose.

Nothing's fair, Pikelet. Some guys get balled at your age, and others – poor ugly bastards – wait till they're thirty. I guess we could give it all back. You wanna give up getting laid, in the interests of fairness?

I shook my head, sheepish.

Just be nice to me, Pikelet.

Orright. I am. I mean I will.

Don't brag about me, okay? Not to Loonie, not to anyone.

I wouldn't, I said with my voice breaking. I promise.

But even while I stood there I saw the pleasure and complacency leaching from her face. She looked down at the grapefruit as though she couldn't remember what it was.

Jesus, she said. Maybe you shouldn't come out again.

What?

It's not right. It's not fair on you.

What if I want to? I asked petulantly.

Listen, Sando will be back soon.

I stared at her. How soon?

The rain's stopped, she said. Go home.

I WAS WIRED night and day for a week. Before this, beyond the desultory appraisal I gave every female I met, I'd had no particular sexual interest in Eva Sanderson. She wasn't quite the stuff of my erotic imaginings. True, she was blonde and confident in that special American way but there was nothing *Playboy* or Hollywood about her. My fantasies lurched from Suzi Quatro to Ali McGraw and back in a moment. The rockin chick, the dark waif. But Eva was stocky and blunt. As a blonde she tended toward the agricultural. She lacked rock-and-roll insouciance on one hand, and on the other she failed to give off the faintest aura of fey sensitivity. If anything she was abrupt and suspicious, handsome rather than pretty. Her limbs were shapely enough though tough and scarred. Yet the idea of her had taken hold. The fact of her body overtook me. Eva was suddenly all I could think about.

I didn't ride out there. Nor did I call her from the box outside the pub. I tried to remember every moment: her belly against mine, the briny taste of her skin, the low, incendiary growl she made. For days the sharp smell of her lingered on my hands and every time I yanked myself under the blankets it seemed to return with the heat of my body. I thought about Sando and what a turd I was to have done this. He might be home any day. I felt the impossibility of the situation coming down on me. I'd buggered everything now, lost it all. And yet I thought again of the bitter, smarting sense of rejection I'd been left with. Sando didn't rate me, didn't give a shit at all. He'd cut me loose. The yellow Brewer was just a consolation prize. He was never my friend. Eva let it slip more than once – we were there to flatter him, to make him feel important. The guru. So the hell with him.

At school lunchbreaks I stood in the phone booth beside the basketball courts and stared at Eva's number etched in blue biro inside my wrist. But I didn't dial it; I didn't dare. Maybe she was serious about my never going back. She might be stricken with remorse. Maybe she'd just felt sorry for me, the boy left behind, and taking me to bed had been some stoned moment of kindness she regretted already. God knows, I hadn't been any good at it. And she could get nasty so quick. If she was off me I should be careful because you never knew what she'd say or do. You couldn't trust her. But it was torment like this, thinking she'd cut me off cold. I wanted her.

When I looked at girls now I compared them to Eva – the shape of their legs, the skinniness of their arms, the way they sheltered their breasts with their shoulders. Their perfumes smelt sugary as cordial. I hated all their rattly plastic bangles, and the way they plastered their zits with prosthetic-pink goo and chewed their lips when they thought no one was looking. Unless every single one of them was lying, they were all going out with older blokes, guys with cars and jobs, men who liked their peroxided fringes and bought them stuff. They suddenly looked so . . . ordinary.

One evening when I thought I heard the chatter of the Volkswagen at the end of the drive, I put down my book and lay very still on the bed. I thought first of Sando, though he'd hardly been gone a fortnight. If it was him, what would he want of me at ten o'clock at night? Unless he knew something. I tried not to think of that, of him here and angry and twice as big as me. Eva wouldn't drive in to try to see me, would she? With my parents asleep in the house? Waiting for me to come out and down the long drive to meet her by the road? The idea was too crazy, too beautiful, too frightening. I snapped off the bed lamp and after a while the engine noise pulled away. I knew well enough what a VW sounded like. Five minutes, it'd been there. It could have been nothing more than a couple of lost Margaret River hippies consulting their map in the mouth of our driveway. Still, I waited to hear it return, barely moved a limb. At the thought of her waiting out in the Kombi my cock began to ache. And then, through the thin wall, the fridge motor kicked in again and I couldn't be sure that I hadn't imagined the entire thing.

I HELD OFF for a whole week. But the next Saturday I rode out in the pelting rain. I felt mad, reckless, doomed.

The dog announced my arrival. Eva came out onto the verandah and didn't say hello. She unzipped my sodden jeans with a determination that bordered on violence, and she took me in her mouth while the dog and the swollen estuary and the whole teeming sky seemed to look on. I held her hair and shivered and cried from relief.

It was over in moments. Eva got up, wiped her face, pulled off the rest of my clothes and took them inside. I followed her to the dryer, saw her sling my stuff in. She wore an old pullover and bellbottom jeans with rainbow-coloured toe-socks. When I reached around to hold her I felt her breasts swinging loose under the wool. The dog sidled in to stare at us.

Thought I told you to stay away, she said.

I pressed myself against her so that she could feel I was still hard. She turned and kissed me. Her mouth tasted starchy. She ran her hands down my back and held me by the buttocks.

Well, she said. Now that you're here.

And so began a pattern. Eva always seemed more vindicated than pleased to see me. Sex was a hungry, impatient business, more urgent for the looming possibility of Sando's unscheduled return. The house had no curtains and few partitions so it was hard not to feel insecure. Sando's dog was a constant and mostly silent witness; it saw me eager, clumsy, exultant, furtive, anxious. That Saturday, it followed us up to the bedroom and watched from the corner as Eva lowered herself on me. Rain drummed on the roof. I was trembling.

You're scared, she said.

No.

Bullshit.

Just cold, I said.

That's okay. Being scared is half the fun. You should know *that* by now.

But I wasn't sure what I knew except that she was silky-hot inside, and strong enough to hold me by the muscles of her pelvis and pin my arms to the bed so that I couldn't have fought her off if I'd wanted to.

We stayed in bed all day as the rain fell and the dog sighed disconsolately. Some time in the afternoon I woke, startled to have slept at all. Eva was watching me. She held my cock as though it was a small bird. With her free hand she stroked my cheek.

I love you, I murmured.

You love getting laid.

No, I mean it.

You don't know *what* you mean.

I lay there, smarting.

I got a postcard from Thailand, she said.

Thailand? Sando.

He's been in Bangkok.

The thought of him now was like a blow. Aren't they in Java? I said, trying to seem breezy.

Something about supplies, she said. Who knows. Now he's talking about the eastern islands.

Which islands?

He didn't say. Lombok, I guess.

Could be any eastern islands.

Yeah, she said with a snort. The Philippines, maybe. Even Hawaii has eastern islands. What an asshole.

So he won't be back straight away.

He's scared of growing old. That's what this shit's about.

The travelling.

All of it. Having his little deputy along for the ride. Loonie's too young and too stupid to be afraid. And Sando loves that, feeds off it. He hates being old.

How old *is* he?

Sando? Thirty-six.

Hell.

You're surprised?

Well, yeah. I mean, he's real fit.

Fit, she said. And lucky.

I reached over to touch her messy knee but she swatted my hand away.

Leave it, she muttered.

Sorry.

We both stared at her scars in silence.

Look at this, she said at last. Can you believe a whole life can come down to a few hunks of fucking bone and gristle?

She got up and limped to the window. Light caught the fine hair of her limbs. I stared at the silhouette-curve of her buttocks.

Why do you let him go? I asked. I don't get it.

Because he needs it, she said.

What about what you need?

He knows what I need, she said with a matter-of-factness that brooked no inquiry. She looked back at me sourly and it seemed to be my cue to leave.

I got out of bed, hoping she'd follow me down to the laundry, but she didn't. I pulled on my still-warm clothes and went back out into the rain.

For a long and ruinous period of my later life I raged against Eva Sanderson, even as I grieved for her. In the spirit of the times I held her morally accountable for all my grown-up troubles. Yet had things proceeded only a little differently – had she been in less pain perhaps, and more clearheaded as a result – maybe we would have wound up friends, made our blunder and let it go, to look upon it afterwards as just another lumpy bit of history. In the seventies the ground seemed to continually slip and change beneath our feet, but Eva knew better than to console herself with a pimply schoolboy. I just wish she'd shown more of an interest in the particular kid she took to bed. God knows, I understand lapses of judgement, the surrender to vanity, the weight of loneliness, for we were both lonely beyond the glow of Sando's attention, and in Sawyer there were so few opportunities for companionship, mutual feeling, shared confidence. But if that's all it had been, a lapse of judgement, one moment of reaching out for comfort, then there might have been so much less to regret.

Although Eva was twenty-five and I was jailbait, I was certain I understood her better than anyone ever would. This was a woman not in the least bit ordinary. As an athlete she'd had very few peers. Like Sando she'd lived at the radical margin of her own sport. There was a warrior spirit in her, an implacable need to win the day. Even if it scared me a little, I understood the contempt she felt for those who withdrew from the fray or settled for something modest or reasonable. It was this conviction, I saw in time, that lay at the heart of her battle with Sando, who'd taken another tack, a mystical path she now said was bullshit. She relished opposition, yet her only real opponents had been the facts of life: gravity, fear, and the limits of endurance. She loved snow the way I loved water – so much it hurt. She didn't want to see snow anymore and most of the time she wouldn't speak of it. But for the best years of her life, years she believed were gone for keeps, she'd trained to fly over it. That was the simple objective, being airborne, up longer, higher, more casually and with more fuckoff elegance than anyone else in the world. I never understood the rules or the science of it but I recognized the singlemindedness it took to match risk with nerve come what may. Such endeavours require a kind of egotism, a near-autistic narrowness. Everything conspires against you – the habits of physics, the impulse to flee – and you're weighed down by every dollop of commonsense ever dished up. Everyone will tell you your goal is impossible, pointless, stupid, wasteful. So you hang tough. You back yourself and only yourself. This idiot resolve is all you have.

Yes, we had some things in common, Eva and I. At twenty-five she was as solipsistic as any teenager, not much better at considering the higher physics than I was. And there was something careless about her that I mistook for courage in the same way I misread Sando's vanity as wisdom. Maybe she was harsh and angry, and hard to like, but I respected her impatience with niceties. Life was too short for rules and obligations. She was all about going hard or going home and if that required cruelty then so be it. At fifteen you can buy such a philosophy.

No, Eva was not ordinary. And neither was the form of consolation she preferred. Given my time over I would *not* do it all again. People talk such a storm of crap about the things they've done, had done to them. The deluded bullshit I've endured in circled chairs on lino floors. She had no business doing what she did, but I'm through hating and blaming. People are fools, not monsters.

Eva had a particular kind of rueful stare, a look she often gave at the end of an afternoon like this rainy Saturday that made me think she'd wearied of me. I always took it as dismissal, as I did this day. I got up and went. But the longer things went on between us, the further we got into our mess, the more frequent and intense those doleful glances became. They were expressions of disgust. I dreaded them. Nowadays, with the distance of the years, I wonder if I misread her. That disgust might have been reserved for herself.

WEEKS WENT BY without further word from Sando and Loonie. A couple of good fronts bore in. I thought about Old Smoky but didn't go. The Brewer stayed in the rain outside the old man's shed. I surfed the Point a couple of times on my stubby little twin-fin and when the Angelus crew nodded or smiled I paddled past with a hauteur as counterfeit as it was unnecessary.

I spent all my free time out at the house with Eva: in the woodshed, the bathtub, the bed. I helped with her rehab exercises and carried shopping up the stairs. In the sack or out in the yard she gave the orders and I was glad to be told. She was spiky and restive yet we still had our laughs. One day we drove out into the forest and ate chicken and drank champagne and made love in the bracken beneath the karris. We played backgammon by the stove on stormy afternoons and fooled with the dog. We made silly paper hats and listened to Captain Beefheart records. A few times I went down on her to the sound of whale songs or Ravi Shankar – it was all the same to me. Now and then she cried for an hour and wouldn't let me touch her. I told her I loved her and I believed it. She pushed me away, drew me back. I was elated, miserable, greedy, grateful. There were afternoons when I retreated to the verandah sick with guilt and an hour later I'd be labouring over Eva's shining back with her hair in my fists. I cowered at the thought of Sando. I uttered his name as a curse in his own bed and she liked it.

During those Saturdays and Sundays with Eva, as autumn quickly became winter, I told my parents the old lies, that I was surfing at the coast or doing jobs for Bill Sanderson and his wife. I was careful to come and go as usual but I'll never know how well I really concealed myself from them. There were moments when I was certain they suspected something amiss, when a glance passed between them at the mention of Sando's name, but I always put it down to my own paranoia and the fact that Loonie's old man had been bitching around town. My absences, after all, were hardly out of the ordinary. I came home on weekend evenings damp-haired and dead tired as ever. I tried not to seem distracted. I refrained from carping about their strange, dowdy habits. I was anxious to make myself inconspicuous. Whether I came home morose or elated I found I could manufacture a deceptively even demeanour. I believed I was alert to their moods, but really my concentration was elsewhere. My mother and father became figures in the background. They'd always been quiet and solicitous but throughout my adolescence and especially during this period they became so insubstantial that I hardly knew them anymore. I didn't know what they thought, what they suspected, what their lives had become. I could only think about Eva.

Eva. I watched her when she was present and conjured her when she was not. She was no longer a girl, but not a woman in the way that my mother was a woman. And I simply couldn't stop looking. At times she basked in the attention, though at other moments she refused to indulge me. When she complained about my dog-eyed stare and waved me away I found ways to watch her without her knowledge. I particularly loved to watch her sleep, for then she was the picture of a body smitten. In sleep she looked thrown down by passion and fatigue. She drooled a little and the tiny thread that glistened on her cheek was like the silver tracks of moisture inside her thighs.

She was taller than me, heavier, stronger. Her bad knee was hotter to the touch than the uninjured one. Her tongue often tasted of cornflakes or the brassiness of painkillers. When she wound her hair into a braid it was a shining hawser, heavy yet supple in my hands. If she was excited or angry there was a wheezy edge to her breath. When she hyperventilated this wheeze of hers had shadow-sounds in it, a multiplicity of breaths.

I watched her so long that I saw her body was a sequence of squares and cubes. Her teeth were square, so were her ears. Her breasts and buttocks were block-like. Even her calf muscles, which squirmed beneath my fingers, had corners. She had wide, blunt hands with square nails and deep ruts at the joints, and her feet were the same. I thought about her shape as I painted her toenails cool green. She pressed one cubic heel against my heart while the other lay playfully in my lap. How I watched her, what a catalogue I made of her movements. I saw her pee, watched her shave her armpits. She said I was a pervert and I wondered if I was.

I knew Eva had a Utah driver's licence and a sheaf of family snaps in her shoulder bag she refused to show me. I was curious about her family, about Salt Lake City, but she was reluctant to talk about any of it. Although I was tempted I never touched her bag or went through her cupboards. I was content to wait until she relented, convinced that she would, and in this, at least, my instincts were vindicated. She told me everything. Indeed there came a time when, to my great consternation, Eva preferred to talk rather than fuck.

EVA TOLD ME how one summer she met Sando on the North Shore of Oahu. She was out from college in California and he was shaping boards for an outfit that shipped them back to the west coast. There was a party at some ramshackle plantation and she liked the look of him, loved the accent, and they got bombed on Maui Wowie and left together. They spent the entire week in her hotel room at Waikiki, which got him sacked from his shaping job, so he followed her to San Francisco until the winter.

Sando didn't much like the cold, and the sea made Eva uneasy but each instinctively recognized the other's obsession. He was older but so strong and lovely. He was glamorous in his sunbleached way. The sex, she felt obliged to tell me, was sensational.

When winter arrived and the Pacific swells returned his surfer friends began to call, and she knew it would only be a matter of time before he flew back to Oahu. Eva tried not to take it hard. It'd been fun, but she had her own season to look to. Snow was falling in the Rockies; every fresh report got her jangly, and before Sando could leave her she caught a plane east. But she couldn't believe how much she missed him. Late that winter, drunk on peppermint schnapps, she phoned him from New Hampshire. Next morning Sando packed a duffle and went to her.

From Hawaii to the snow. It was quite a move for Sando. She taught him to ski – downhill and cross-country – which kept him fit and sane, and she even found him a Snurfer, the closest thing to a surfboard she could offer him up there in the mountains, but she never expected to win him away from the sea for long. They made love and drank hard and dropped acid, never talking about his own stalled career until the season was over, and by then she said he'd gone all Van Morrison on her.

They summered in Malibu where half the surfers were junkies and the whole scene made him sick. He got reading and took on new ideas about diet and training regimes and meditation. When it came to training Eva still preferred the party method. Sando said she relied on bravado more than technique. He told her she travelled on pure entitlement, not achievement. There was an almighty blow-up and she threw him out. He slept on the beach, surfed, ran all day. She took him back and got fit. He worked her hard.

Next winter he travelled with her as coach as well as lover. His mental discipline fortified her. And she flourished. She went from being a gifted but lazy competitor at the fringe, just another moneyed dilettante, to becoming a serious name. Periodically Sando flew to Hawaii or drove down to Baja for waves. She understood how he needed it. He came back brown and scarred and happy. Those days, said Eva, they were the life.

In those days freestyle skiers were the wild bunch, a scene unto themselves. At night they got drunk and skied off chalet roofs, attempting whole alpine villages, skidding rooftop to rooftop. They skied bridges and the guardrails of mountain roads. They bounced off cars and plummeted down sketchy ravines. In aerial com-petition they scared the shit out of people. Because nobody would insure them, theirs was still an amateur circuit; they were like mad-dog skateboarders. People dreamed about a World Cup and sanctioned events at the Olympics, but the skiing establishment was welded to tradition. The old-school was about keeping your feet on the ground and looking sophisticated – a European thing; a martini and Ingrid Bergman deal – whereas hotdoggers wanted to rock and roll, to get some air, to be upside down, to be scary-good rather than just pretty. People said they were nuts, brats, wreckers, degenerates. And they were right, said Eva fondly – we kicked ass.

The same day she fell at the Intermountain, a guy from Montana broke his neck, and although she'd never believed such pain was possible she realized she'd gotten off lightly. Unlike the other guy, she wouldn't be drinking through a straw the rest of her life. You could put a knee back together. But the reconstruction was botched and after the second unsuccessful attempt there was, thanks to her father, a lawsuit. Which was when everything began to unravel. In Utah new avenues of litigation were plotted, but things got ugly between Sando and the old man and Eva began to feel like a medico-legal experiment. There was a vicious quarrel and the couple flew out to Australia in the hope of some respite. Sando took her west where he'd surfed in the sixties. They bought a piece of coastal bush and he started building a house but before he could finish it Eva convinced herself she was better and they flew back across the Pacific for the new season. But the knee hadn't come right. The first moment she was back in skis she sensed weakness, but told herself she'd manage. Yet it only takes a sliver of doubt to make you vulnerable. When you're fifty feet in the air your only armour is conviction. Regardless of how hard you've trained, the moment your self-belief wavers, you are in danger. And because she was anxious she hurried slightly. That's all it took – rushing the manoeuvre – and she nearly got away with it. But the landing was heavy and unbalanced, so that one leg took the bulk of the impact – wrong angle, wrong leg – and the knee collapsed. She cannoned, wailing, into the crowd. She hadn't skied since.

Eva said that the moments before she landed were her last happy ones. I didn't want to believe her, but she was adamant. She wanted me to understand. Being airborne. Sky and snow the same colour. Her skis a defiant cross against the milky blur.

When she spoke about those ghostly, quiet moments she wasn't bitter or wistful, but the awe in her voice unnerved me.

I miss being afraid, she said. That's the honest truth.

IN TIME THERE WAS neither much sex nor talk to be had at Eva's. We smoked hash and gazed out at the rain and I wondered if she'd decided that she'd already said too much. For a while there'd been such angry, urgent passion and then a lightness between us, as though Eva's rage had subsided. It was then that I got to know her better, when she began to tell me about herself; I felt I'd been chosen all over again. I was enlarged by her trust. It felt like love – or friendship at least. But our fellow-feeling grew thin. Eva became restless again, and mean along with it. She needled me, she seethed and provoked. She took more pills, smoked so much hash she seemed absent half the time. If she looked my way she made no effort to disguise her indifference. Those rare occasions when she took me back into her bed she shouted Sando's name in my face. We fucked until I was in pain and she was in tears.

One Saturday morning, after such an unhappy encounter, she got out of bed to go to the bathroom and when she returned I saw the shape of her belly. There was a new tilt to her pelvis. She saw me staring.

What?

Nothing.

I'm puffy, she said.

Nah.

It happens every month.

Really?

Jesus, Pikelet, don't you know anything?

No, I conceded miserably. I don't know anything.

Poor baby.

Well, I know you're bored with me.

Yeah, she said. But it's not really your fault.

I felt tears coming. I clenched my teeth against them.

Listen, she said as though offering me a lifeline. I have a game we can play.

FROM THE BOTTOM OF the wardrobe she brought out a strap and a pink cellophane bag. The strap had a collar and a sliding brass ring. I snorted nervously, waiting for the joke, but Eva handled these new props with a reverence that brought a falling sensation to the pit of my guts.

I don't get it, I said.

I'll show you, she murmured.

What if I don't want to?

Then I'll be disappointed, I guess.

Eva sat on the bed beside me. She drew the leather across her thigh while I lay there considering the likely ramifications of her disappointment.

So, I said. Show me.

You know how to hyperventilate, right?

I nodded warily.

Well, it's kinda like that.

I looked at the padded collar and the brass ring that did the work of a slipknot. From where I lay I could smell the sweat and perfume in the leather.

You *hang* yourself?

Sure. Sometimes.

Fuck. Why?

Because I like it.

But why do you like it?

Because, little man, she said flipping it at me playfully. It makes me come like a freight train.

Far out, I muttered.

She smiled. I tried to take it in.

So, how do you know when to stop?

Practice, I guess. You should know.

Me? Gimme a break.

Come on, Pikelet, she said soothingly. I've heard you guys talk. Spots, stars, tunnel vision.

You want me to . . . hang myself?

No.

Well, there's no way.

Of course not.

So, what then? What d'you want me to do?

Eva became girlish for a moment. She put her fingers through my hair.

I just want you to watch.

Geez, Eva.

It feels better; I can't tell you.

I dunno.

And it's safer. Like having a dive buddy.

I sat up in bed, anxious and revolted. I hated the sharp leather smell already.

I can't, I said. You shouldn't ask me.

She sighed. Okay. Sure.

Eva swept her props off the bed and began to dress. I felt the sudden weight of her disappointment. The day was over already. I'd be home early.

I'm sorry, I said.

Sure, she murmured, pulling on a tee-shirt.

It's just —

I'll make do on my own, Pikelet. I'm a big girl.

But it's not safe.

Well, no guts no glory, huh?

Sensing that I'd been dismissed already, I watched her rake a brush through her hair.

What'll you do?

I have a mirror, she said, misunderstanding me. I can watch myself.

Does Sando do this with you?

She turned back to consider me.

I don't have to answer that.

But how did it start?

I'm not going to answer that either.

She grabbed the end of the rumpled sheet as though she might yank it off me. I caught the ravishing curve of her breasts beneath the tee-shirt and felt a rush of panic at the idea of being cut off from her.

I don't want you to kill yourself, I said.

I won't. Not if you don't let me.

I took a handful of the sheet and jerked it so hard that she staggered a little. Her bad leg gave way and she braced herself against the bed. I reached up beneath her shirt and held her breasts and we stared at each other a moment before she took down her pants and lowered herself to me.

I love you, I whispered.

We'll see.

But not the belt.

Okay, honey. We hardly need it.

She pulled her shirt up and put a nipple to my lips and I fixed on it greedily, certain that I'd won a moral victory. But once we'd raised a sweat Eva disentangled herself, reached down beside the bed and brought up the cellophane bag.

I wasn't much of a partner in her game. I was mostly the audience, little more than a bit of bodyweight and a steady pair of hands. There were whale songs on the stereo now – otherworldly moans and clicks and squeaks. Eva lay on the pillow and pulled me back into her until we were panting again and then she pulled the bag over her face like a hood, twisting it tight against her throat so that it filled and shrank with every breath. The plastic was pink and translucent and behind it Eva's features looked all out of focus. Pretty soon the bag fogged up and I could only see the contours of her nose and chin and the deep indentation of her mouth with each indrawn breath. She worked hard to get air. A sheen of sweat lay across her sternum and her labouring neck and the shine became beads and then runnels while the ghostly whales rumbled and squealed in the house around us. At her signal I did what I'd been told to do. I lay on her chest. And then I gently throttled her.

Before she began to shudder I thought of boys falling to the ground in swoons. Mottled faces. Blue-white lips. The stiffened limbs of the poleaxed. Like steers given the bolt in the killing yard. And I remembered the way all sound and light shrank to the fineness of copper wire.

The muscles of Eva's pelvis twitched and clamped and I came before I saw that she'd lost consciousness, before I tore the bag away, before I even let go her neck. Only the dog stirred me into action. I didn't even hear the poor creature come in but something had roused it from slumber down beside the stove for it was suddenly there on the bed, growling and butting and snapping at my arms.

The bag came away with a hank of Eva's hair. She was white-eyed and drenched. Her neck rippled with tiny tremors and I began to shout over the mad, scrabbling dog.

Eva! Breathe!

I was fifteen years old and afraid. Sex was, once

more, a confounding mystery. I didn't understand love or even physiology. I was so far out of my depth it frightens me now to recall it. Yes, I was scared but not nearly scared enough. I didn't understand just how perilous Eva's predicament was. With the dog there I didn't dare slap her or shake her. I simply yelled.

There was, at last, a snagging noise deep in her head. It was not unlike the sound the old man made in the middle of the night. Then there came a gasping spasm. Eva's arms flew out so hard and suddenly that I took a blow to the ear. Her legs jerked. She began to whoop in air.

I KNEW EVA was expecting me but I didn't go back next day. Instead I got up early, limp with fatigue, and wandered through the forest in the misting rain. No one was about and I was grateful because I was a mess. The longer I walked and the hungrier and tireder I got, the angrier I became.

I'd been an idiot; I saw it now. It wasn't Eva's fault her life had gone the way it had, and I didn't blame her for whatever it was that she couldn't or wouldn't explain. She was what she was and I loved her. But I couldn't kid myself it was mutual. She might require me now, but she didn't love me. It had only been a matter of weeks but already I couldn't think how it had begun. Had it been an accident, this thing between us, or did she plan it, right down to the advent of the cellophane bag? And why me? Because Sando wouldn't play her game? He was a hellman but maybe there were things he just wouldn't do – and here I was, too young and stupid to refuse her. How could he hold out so long? Eva Sanderson was not an easy person to deny. Did he resist out of love, or from discipline? Either way I admired him for this at least. I loved his wife. And I wished he'd come home and save me from her.

I called her from school on Monday and at first she was peevish and then she cried. I'd rung to say it was over, that I couldn't come out anymore, but I couldn't get it said. By the time I hung up I felt like a bastard for making her cry.

Next day the VW was out on the street at lunchtime in the shade beyond the gym. My heart jerked at the sight of it.

I'm sorry, Eva said when I drew up to her window.

I'm sorry too, I murmured.

Let's go for a drive, huh?

I looked over my shoulder a moment. There were kids kicking a Fanta can across the netball courts.

I've only got half an hour.

Sure. Get in.

We drove to the war memorial and looked out across the sound and all its islands and bays and sat for a time in silence. It seemed to me that she was working her way up to saying something important. And then she reached across and put a hand in my lap.

You're kind to me.

Kind?

Nobody's as kind as you, Pikelet.

Really?

Really.

She unbuttoned my pants and drew out my aching cock and went down on me there in the noonday carpark. Within ten minutes I was back at school.

I DIDN'T CALL AGAIN all week but when Saturday came around I rode straight out to Eva's. The dog seemed leery of me but she was smiling.

I feel like walking, she said. You want to hike?

What about your leg?

I want to push it some.

Well, I said. If you reckon.

We hiked out across the wooded hills toward the cliffs with the dog darting ahead. There were no roads. We were unlikely to meet anybody out there but it was careless of us. Eva seemed relaxed. Her limp was only slight when we set out but by the time we got to the ridge overlooking Old Smoky she was in real pain.

You okay?

Fine.

It doesn't look good.

I said it's fine.

But we stopped at the edge of the windswept ridge and went no further. I stared out at the bombora, that day just a dark, intermittent lumping of swells in the distance.

Kinda stupid thing to do, huh?

Walk here, you mean?

No, dummy. Paddle out there a mile to go surfing. Alone.

Yeah.

But I guess you need it.

She was right but I didn't respond. I didn't really want to talk about it.

I understand you, Pikelet. And I understand Sando. But he's never had anything precious taken away.

Eva —

But you, she said taking my hand. You're different. I can see it in your face. You've got this look. Like you're expecting to lose something – everything – every moment.

When she took my hand I felt electrified. I wanted to pull down her jeans and spread her legs and reach into her. I wanted to press her against the stony ground and fuck her until she called out my name. But she kept on talking and nothing happened and I stood there throbbing and half listening until she was yanking my arm and saying c'mon, let's go back.

Halfway home she couldn't walk anymore. Her face was white. For a while she leant against me, bracing, hopping, until even that was too much and I was forced to piggyback her across the wild, uneven country. The first few seconds, when she hitched up and clamped her thighs around my waist and pushed her breasts tight to my back, I was delirious with pride and lust and a stupid sense of triumph. In my mind I was carrying her home like some warrior prince. She rested her hot cheek against my neck and I could smell the pear scent of her hair as I stepped it out. But the feeling only lasted a minute. She was heavy. I remembered how far it was to the house.

By the time we got to her place I was spent. The sky was black with impending rain. The dog trailed us listlessly into the yard and slumped into the undercroft while I levered Eva the last few feet up the stairs.

She snatched her pills and the hash pipe and lay back on the sofa until she could speak again.

You're right, she said. Right to expect it all to be snatched away from you, Pikelet. Because it will be. It can be. And hey, maybe it should be.

I didn't like the tone of her voice. I figured I'd better go.

But I stayed. We took a bath together like people in the movies. We smoked a little hash and climbed into bed and when her plastic bag came out I did my best to please her.

For a week or two Eva came by the school or I wagged classes and met her on the wharf so we could drive out to lonely beaches. We grew more reckless and impulsive and so tired that when we weren't at each other we were bitching like married people. And on weekends, despite myself, I strangled her.

I hated it. In time I saw that for her everything else was mere courting, payment for what she really wanted. I hated the evil, crinkly sound of the bag and the smeary film of her breath inside it. I came to hate all masks and hoods and drawn faces without features and in retrospect I see that I probably hated Eva as well.

SOMEBODY ONCE told me I was a classical addictive personality. I laughed at her. She threw a plastic cup of water in my face and I sat there smiling at the thousand cuts down the inside of her arms. Staff appeared around us crisp and silent as ghosts.

When I was born, I said, I took a breath and wanted more. I found my mother's nipple and sucked. I liked that. I wanted more. That's called being human.

I know what you are, the woman murmured.

Yes, I said. You're the expert.

They led her away to dinner and I sat there alone with my sneer as the tears leaked out of me.

THE LAST sucking bubble of consciousness. The rising gorge of panic. Yes, a delicious ricochet of sparks.

I suppose I knew well enough what it felt like. It was intense, consuming, and it could be beautiful. That far out at the edge of things you get to a point where all that stands between you and oblivion is the roulette of body-memory, the last desperate jerks of your system trying to restart itself. You feel exalted, invincible, angelic because you're totally fucking poisoned. Inside it's great, feels brilliant. But on the outside it's squalid beyond imagining.

As a kid I didn't know what respiratory acidosis was, nor could I even begin to comprehend the sheer unpredictability of premature ventricular contractions and the manner in which they can shunt a body into cardiac arrest. I was as dim and horny as any other schoolboy, a sucker for excitement, and I'd been scaring the shit out of myself since primary school, but each time I let go Eva's throat and ripped the slimy bag off her face I didn't see rapture. What I saw was death ringing her like a bell.

So I began to deceive her. I had to. I'd come to resent Eva Sanderson but I didn't want her to die. And I certainly didn't want to be the patsy left behind, the fool calling the ambulance, the one whose fingermarks were up and down her neck like hickeys. I was scared to the point where I couldn't even get it up anymore, so I began to fake it. In the end I was faking it all. She saw to herself anyway; she was on automatic by then.

When she wanted me to choke her I learnt that I could brace myself on my elbows, give her a sense of my body on hers, without letting my full weight down. When I held her throat I made all the noise of exertion while applying less and less pressure. I slipped my fingers under the bag to break the seal. I blew air across her face while pretending to shout at her. Sometimes

I didn't even touch her throat at all. I held my palms over her neck and asked her could she feel it, could she feel it, and she felt it because she expected it, because I was there and she expected it. She was blind in her foggy bag, intoxicated by the idea of what she was doing, and I hovered, palms down, like some kind of boy-shaman, willing life into her, holding off the shivering darkness.

I wonder if she ever knew. She did become more and more irritable, as if sex no longer satisfied her. Once when I began to giggle at how stupid we looked, how ludicrous it was to be lurching and growling about like this while the dog scratched at the door, she slapped me so hard that I rode home and lay on my narrow bed and shouted at my mother to please turn the bloody vacuum off and get a life.

I faked it. I wanted her, wanted to be free of her. Yet I was afraid of her. And afraid for her. I was trapped. It was as if some mighty turbulence had hold of me, and nothing – not even Sando's return – would ever rescue me.

But something did come. A bolt of indigo lightning. The livid vein that had begun to fork across Eva's tight belly. You couldn't mistake it. Not even I was so dense as to miss it.

I was on the bed one afternoon, spent and full of

loathing, when she limped up naked from the steaming bathroom, a towel coiled on her head. It was right there in front of me.

Eva, I said. You're pregnant.

Something in her face gave way. She ricked the towel down and tied it about her waist. In a few more weeks she'd need a bigger towel.

I was fixing to tell you.

Really?

Go home, she murmured. The fun's over now.

Fuck, I said. Fuck you.

C'mon, she murmured. You knew it had to stop somewhere. I can't do this shit with a baby coming.

Is it mine?

Don't be absurd.

I tried to count back but I didn't even know which numbers I required.

I can't believe it.

Well, believe it. It's true.

Even as I lay there I felt my shock becoming relief. Not so much that the child was not mine, but that I'd been delivered. A new force had stepped in to present her with a defining choice.

Eva went back down to the bathroom and wiped the steam-fog from the mirror and brushed out her hair while I stood in the doorway to watch. I considered her wide shoulders and broad back, her narrow waist, the square, womanly buttocks and the way she favoured one leg even while dragging a brush through her long, wet hair. I felt strangely bashful, as though we'd been restored to our proper roles. Here I was again, a visitor in her house, a schoolboy standing unbidden in the doorway to a grown woman's bathroom. The plain light of Saturday afternoon was everywhere in the house.

You want me to chop some wood?

No, she said. Thank you. Go home.

On Sunday I surprised my father by joining him at the back fence to slash the winter weeds and burn what couldn't be hacked down. He seemed hesitant, almost fearful in my company. At day's end as we tended the smouldering edges of the firebreak with bag and hose he cleared his throat and spoke.

I had Loonie's old man here yesterday.

Oh, yeah? I said.

You know he's not my sort of fella.

I know what you mean.

But he's been talking about the people you see out the coast. Says Loonie's gone off the deep end. Won't listen to reason. Son, he used to be your mate.

Yes, I said.

I don't understand it. But I don't think you should go out there anymore.

I nodded. If you like.

He smiled and I felt cheap about how easy this was

to concede to him when a month ago I would have told him to mind his own business.

Good boy, he said, wiping ash across his stubbled chin. Good lad.

LITTLE MORE than a week later Sando returned. He came running out from the BP servo in Sawyer and I nearly shat myself. He looked dark and grizzled and happy.

Hey, he said. I'm gunna be a father.

Far out, I said. I thought she looked different.

Incredible, eh.

Yeah. Man, congratulations.

We shook hands awkwardly.

Shit, he said, holding my hand with a grip just short of painful. You chopped a bloody lot of wood out there, mate.

Well, I said. Not much swell.

Didn't want you to think I don't notice these things.

I laughed uncertainly. I couldn't read him. I wondered if the smudgy bruises on Eva's neck had lingered, or if I'd left something out there to give myself away. It occurred to me later they could have fessed up to one another about their weeks apart, and perhaps this was their way.

Hey, how was the trip? I stammered.

Lively.

Did you get waves?

Jesus, we got everything. Seasick, shot at, seen off, spiderbitten, infected, deported. And yeah, honkin waves.

Haven't seen Loonie, I said.

You and me both.

You mean he's not back?

Little prick blew me off. Took a boat to Nias.

What happened?

Didn't wanna come home, I spose.

Man.

Wilful little bastard, isn't he? Fuckin nuts, actually.

At that moment Fat Bob the mechanic sidled out from the shadows of his workshop. Sando slapped me on the shoulder.

Hey, keep an eye on the weather. We'll do Old Smoky, eh?

Orright.

Gotta go. Come out sometime.

Okay, I'll do that.

But we never surfed Old Smoky together again. Nor did I visit his place while he was there. I did my best to stay away.

There are spring days down south when all the acacias are pumping out yellow blooms and heady pollen and the honeyeaters and wattlebirds are manic with their pillaging and the wet ground steams underfoot in the sunshine and you feel fresher and stronger than you are. Yes, the restorative force of nature. I can vouch for its value – right up to the point of complete delusion. I go down sometimes on leave to cut the weeds and burn off the way my father did, to surf the Point and collect my frazzled wits. But I've learnt not to surrender to swooning spring. In spring you can really ease off on yourself, and when that happens you'll believe anything at all. You start feeling safe. And then pretty soon you feel immune. Winters are long in Sawyer. A bit of sunshine and nectar goes straight to your head.

I saw Eva in the general store. It was October and she was in a long skirt and sandals. She stood in the narrow aisle considering a bin full of mousetraps. She was fuller in the face and her hair was held back with barrettes. At the sight of her pot belly I felt a tiny stab of lust. I wheeled around and heard her say my name as I slipped out of the shop and into the sleepy street.

In November Frank Loon confronted Sando in the street and took a swing at him but the younger man was too quick. There was a bit of push and shove outside the bank during which Mister Loon uttered threats. From then on it seemed that Sando and Eva did their shopping thirty miles away in Angelus.

I wasn't sleeping much. Some nights I got up and slipped out to the old man's shed to sharpen his tools. One morning my mother found me asleep out there with the axe at my feet. She asked me if I had some troubles but I said that I didn't. I probably thought I was telling her the truth.

I rode out to the coast some weekends to surf. Several times I hiked up behind Sando's place to hide in the peppy scrub and watch the house. I stayed downwind for fear of alerting the dog and though it found me one time it didn't give me away. I saw Eva pegging out laundry in the sun, saw the shine of her bare belly, saw the bras and undies she was hanging up and felt like a dirty schoolboy for watching. I had an urge to wait a while until no one was about and then creep down to press my face into her damp underthings or slip beneath the house and beat off at the thought of her swollen breasts. But I never did.

I all but failed that year of school and I was shamed by the haunted look on my mother's face. The school report recommended that I leave and seek a trade apprenticeship, but I told her I'd stay on and get my act right. Over the Christmas holidays I found every book on next year's syllabus and read late into the night while the old man snored and stopped, snored and stopped, like a man grinding away with a blade at a whetstone.

THE NEW YEAR was weeks old when I found myself surfing beside Sando one morning at the Point. Bareback in nothing but his Speedos, he was noseriding an old tanker from the fifties. He looked fit and tanned as he kicked the board out of the wave and settled down beside me.

Pikelet, he said.

What's with the budgie-smugglers? I asked.

Dog ate the arse out of my boardies. Anyway, what's wrong with Speedos? Son, they made this nation what it is.

You're scarin people.

Well, he said. They need a little scarin round here.

We paddled out together and waited for a set.

How you been? he asked.

Yeah, good, I lied.

Startin to think you're avoidin us.

Well, I said. School and stuff.

You heard from Loonie? he asked, kind enough not to point out that we were in the midst of the summer holidays.

No, I said. Not a word.

Man, what a disappointment he turned out to be.

I spose.

Mate, I thought he was the real deal, y'know? The man not-ordinary.

Maybe ordinary's not so bad, I offered.

Pikelet, you gotta get outta this fuckin town.

I shrugged.

Come and see us, you dick.

I caught a wave in and walked up the hot sand to where Eva lay in the sun with a book. She wore a ragged straw hat and her hair was glossy and her skin was tanned as I'd never seen before. She cut quite a figure in a polka dot bikini. Her breasts were huge and her belly shone. Her distended navel was like a fruit stalk. When she saw me she hoisted herself to her feet. I took in the lavish sway of her back and smiled.

Gross, huh?

No, I said, conscious of passing bathers. No, it's beautiful.

Jesus.

No, honest.

You really *are* a pervert, she said with unexpected tenderness.

Takes one to know, I said, grinning sadly.

We're leaving, Pikelet. After the baby comes.

Oh, I said. I should have been relieved but I felt a twist of panic and it must have shown.

D'you really mind so much?

I picked wax from the deck of my battered twin-fin.

Pikelet?

Can I see you? I asked without looking up.

Oh, baby. No.

Just once. Please?

Pikelet.

You owe it to me, I said without properly understanding what kind of threat I'd uttered.

Shit, Pikelet.

I'll leave you alone. Just once.

I never would have blown the whistle on her – I couldn't have done it – but for her at least this must have been real and present danger.

Yeah, she said so bitterly that it felt like a blow. For old times' sake, right?

On a Thursday while Sando was in Angelus I rode out there and was met by the dog. Eva wouldn't let me upstairs so we went without preamble into the shadows of the undercroft where the smells of soil and wax and fibreglass were all about us. I knelt and lifted her dress and kissed the hard projection of her belly while she ran her hands abstractedly through my hair. Her breasts were long and heavy and between her legs everything felt fat and wet and ripe.

Hurry, she said.

I'm sorry, I murmured.

Yeah, well, we're both sorry now.

She turned and braced against the workbench and we took it slowly and carefully. I held her gorgeous belly and saw the veins stand proud in her neck and the sweat gather on her back and when it was over neither of us pretended to be happy.

I NEVER SAW THE BABY. In February the old man copped a flying belt at the mill. The initial report made it seem like a let-off – it could easily have been a walking blade or worse, and there were no severed limbs. But when Mum and I got to the hospital in Angelus we saw that half his face was mashed and they told us he'd suffered a major skull fracture from the steel beam he'd been thrown against. Nobody's fault, just a freak accident.

He never regained consciousness.

Eva had her baby in the same hospital while Dad was there. A boy, or so I heard. Eva and the child were long gone by the time the old man died. We buried him in the pioneer cemetery back along the river. His mates from the mill came. Frank Loon was there but the Sandersons stayed away. They may have already left town.

My father's death hit me with a force that felt targeted and personal. I felt chastised by it and it really pulled me up. Afterwards, Mum looked at me fearfully, as though I was a stranger. Now I knew there was no room left in my life for stupid risks. Death was everywhere – waiting, welling, undiminished. It would always be coming for me and for mine and I told myself I could no longer afford the thrill of courting it.

Driven by loneliness and remorse and a desire to compensate my mother somehow, I put all my energies into study. I didn't surf much and I kept to myself to the extent of being thought a weirdo. My last two years of school were empty and desperate, but through a regimen that relied more on hard discipline than intellectual curiosity, I dragged myself from the bottom of the class and began to make headway. Eventually my marks were excellent, but my heart wasn't in it.

People said the old man's death was the beginning of the end for the mill and they were only half wrong – it reeled from crisis to crisis for another decade. Mum got a modest payout, which left her free and clear with the house as well as a pension. She saved enough to put me through university and I did my best to be a dutiful son. She never accused me of having forsaken the old man for Bill Sanderson or abandoned her for Eva, though I couldn't have blamed her if she had. I'd absented myself from their lives so long and the unspoken hurt from it lingered for years.

We tried to find some closeness, Mum and I. I wrote every week from the city and phoned her every few days. I drove home some weekends and at semester breaks I stayed weeks at a time. I tried to show I loved her but our relationship was a polite, undeclared failure – there was tenderness but no intimacy – and in this regard it could have been a rehearsal for marriage.

At twenty, after years of barely surfing at all, I went to Bali and finally saw the cave at Uluwatu. I climbed down through it to the sea and surfed the big, winding lefthander for an hour, amped but totally out of condition. I had a bad fall, blew a disc in my back. It took me a week to get home to Perth and when I did I went to pieces. The prolapse sorted itself out soon enough but I had a kind of breakdown. I was only a few weeks from finishing my degree. I never returned to see it through. Instead I holed up in a caravan on a sheep station and put myself back together as best I knew how.

GRACE ANDREWS loved me. Even after she grew wary, there was that to remember. She taught in the zoology department of the university where I worked as a lab technician. My mother adored her, was overjoyed when we married, and I was euphoric, never happier in my life. We had two daughters, so beautiful I could never stop being anxious for them. And now they're women, old enough to find me more an amusement than a puzzle.

When Grace was pregnant she said I was weird about it. Men, she said, were supposed to be turned off by all that fluid, the gross belly, the big backside and puffy ankles. *That* was normal.

I laughed. I really thought she was joking.

So you prefer revulsion to reverence?

A girl doesn't mind reverence, she quipped. But reverent lust is another thing.

What can you mean? I asked, still grinning.

Well, it's creepy.

Ah. Yes. Creepy.

There was yet a hint of laughter in our voices but I was unnerved by the exchange. Years later, when it shouldn't have mattered anymore, I made the mistake of returning to this conversation as I dropped the girls home one Sunday afternoon. There'd been a photo of an actress naked and pregnant on the cover of a glamour magazine, which sparked a surprising furore. To my mind it was a rather brave and beautiful image, but I was curious about what Grace might think. She seemed annoyed that I'd even bring it up.

Grotesque, she said, as the girls hauled their bags up the steps to her door. Now they're mainstreaming porn.

Okay, I murmured.

I leant against the car, conscious of the potential for things to go unhelpfully sour. Perhaps it was stupid of me to mention it. I was no great success as a man but I had been, I thought, a faithful, gentle husband. Never sexually insistent, I steered clear of oddness. I took no interest in pornography. I made myself quite safe and ordinary – a lab bloke, a threat to nobody. And yet.

I gave a wave and got back in the car.

Nobody wants to be creepy. I was careful, always backing off. And somehow, somewhere along the track, I went numb. I couldn't say what it was and didn't dare try. How do you explain the sense of being made to feel improper? I withdrew into a watchful rectitude, anxious to please, risking nothing. I followed the outline of my life, carefully rehearsing form without conviction, like a bishop who can't see that his faith has become an act.

I started, despite myself, to fool with electricity. A couple of times I came to on the tile floor at work, down beneath the sinks and benches where the odours of agar and disinfectant and formaldehyde brewed like some obscene secret, and the return of consciousness brought with it a sad blankness like the lingering melancholy after sex.

I didn't understand this behaviour. I had no special interest in electricity. Granted, it's a potent, tangible presence in a world that's cast off presences. It was just a moment of righteous sensation, like a blow to the head. It knocked me down. It hurt like hell. But it was something I could feel.

IN A DENTIST'S waiting room, during a year I can barely recall, I came upon a photo of Bill Sanderson in a travel magazine. It seems he'd come to preside over quite an empire. Snowboards, alpine apparel – all dripping rebel chic. The interview mentioned his wife Eva and their son Joseph – a good Mormon name. There was much talk of risk in the financial sense. Sando was a kind of investment guru, a motivational speaker of some note. Out on the Aspen slopes he looked like a grizzly, sunbleached Kris Kristofferson, a man arrived.

It was my mother who sent the news clipping about Eva Sanderson. I still don't know why she did. Until that moment I never gave her sufficient credit to imagine she might take some little pleasure in passing it on. But the chances are she simply thought I'd like to know.

Without the slightly lurid details and the connection to Utah wealth, Eva's death might have gone unreported. In any event it earned only two inches of a Reuters column. Eva was found hanging naked from the back of a bathroom door in Portland, Oregon. A Salvadorean hotel employee discovered her with a belt around her neck. The deceased had been the sole occupant of her five-star room, the cause of death cardiac arrest as a result of asphyxiation.

There was no one I could talk to, least of all my mother. Grace found the clipping and wanted, with good cause, to know what it signified. But I couldn't say. I wouldn't risk setting off the rolling mass of trouble inside me. I choked it down. At quite some cost.

You couldn't blame Grace for how things went. She just wanted to be happy. She had her career to look to, and she was anxious for the girls. And in the end I wasn't fit. No question about that.

Afterwards I had myself put away for a spell. I only signed myself out to go to my mother's funeral, a day of hard and vivid feeling. I took the burial as a sacrament of my own failure as much as a tribute to my gentle mother's life. My girls were there. They seemed happy to see me and I couldn't hold their wariness against them. Grace left her new bloke at home though she needn't have. I would have behaved. She seemed wistful but determined and it clearly upset her to see me looking the way I did. I had a few scars by then and I was woozy with pills. I felt the hopeless tug of love as she led the girls towards the car. The mourners around me were careful but not afraid. I have never been a violent man. Just a little creepy, it seems.

I didn't go back to the hospital. I broke an undertaking. Got in a car and drove east, as far away from the sea and the city as possible.

WHEN I WAS on the ward there was a tall, reedy bloke who carried a bible with him all day. He had a habit of fixing on things you said during group work and hitting you later with a few pithy verses to be going on with. He had me down as some kind of compulsive – not miles off the mark – but I wanted to pull his ears off when he told me that a man who even thinks about having his neighbour's wife is already an adulterer.

No, Desmond, I told him. Bullshit.

Can't deny it!

You get ideas. We all get ideas. Thoughts. And most of them come and go without causing anybody grief.

Desmond shook his head and I wanted to get him by the hair, squeeze the poison from his head. *Wanted to*, but didn't. I told him he was sad and dangerous, that he shouldn't say such things, especially not to vulnerable people like us. I was well and truly wigged out at the time, but still sane enough to know there's a world of difference between thinking things and doing them.

You lack morality, he said mildly enough.

You call that morality? I said, trying not to shout. Robbing people of the distinction between thoughts and actions?

Sport, said Desmond, I tell you this out of love. You are a captive of evil.

Talk like that frightened me because in an unsteady moment you could believe it. I was tired and sad and fucked up but I wasn't going to give in to bullshit. I'd been prey to false convictions aplenty and I'd had enough. It *is* possible to believe that as an idea comes into your mind, an act has been born and there's nothing you can do about it. It's as if thinking something causes it to happen, makes an action inevitable, even necessary. Sometimes it's good to remind yourself it isn't so.

A captive of evil, said Desmond.

No, I said. I'm a voluntary patient.

What I didn't say, because I didn't trust myself not to clock him one, is that nobody should be a slave to their thoughts – this was captivity, this was evil.

All about there were others watching Desmond and me, waiting for a blow-up. There were people in our midst who believed that babies had died and cities burnt because of thoughts they'd had.

Do you lust after your neighbour's wife? asked the girl with the slashed arms. Really, she said drolly, you can tell us.

My *wife*, I said. My wife is now my neighbour's wife. And my old neighbour's wife is dead.

Man, that's fucked up, said someone.

No lust?

Not much, I said. Not now.

LOONIE DIED in Mexico, shot in a bar in Rosarito, not far from Tijuana. Some kind of drug deal gone bad. Maybe he did business with the wrong cops. For years stories had made their way back to me, sightings on the northern beaches of Sydney or in Peru or the Mentawais. His reputation for fearlessness endured. He surfed hard and lived hard and seemed to finance it all with drug scams and smuggling. It was said he bought his way out of Indonesia several times, that he had contacts in the TNI. I wonder about his apprenticeship to Sando, how much more than just surfing it might have involved – all those side-trips to Thailand, the long, unexplained absences, surfboards arriving from all over the globe – and whether Sando's family money had been augmented by his darker business interests.

I felt a pang when I heard about Loonie. It hardly sent me into a spin the way Eva's death had, but I felt hollow, as though there was suddenly less of me.

From a call box in Wiluna, surrounded by broken glass and red dirt, I called Grace.

I'm sorry to call, I said.

Yeah, you probably are.

Everyone I know is dead. Or gone.

And what are you planning to do?

Put it all behind me, I said like a politician. I'm gunna put it all behind me and move on.

She hung up on me.

FOR A WHILE I shared a humpy with a defrocked priest. He was an alcoholic and a wise man and for a time I hated him. I'd only come asking for water for my car's boiling radiator but he saw this was the least of my problems. It was obvious he'd never lost his missionary zeal because he hid the keys to my car for three weeks until I climbed back into my own skin.

We lived beside a dry salt lake that rippled and swam against itself all day. Parched and cracked as it was, it seemed the lake was always full, never really empty at all. Long after I straightened out and he gave me back my keys, I stayed on – six months in the end. The old man slept inside on a steel cot and I rolled out my swag under the pulsing stars on the dry lakebed. During the day we sat in the ragged shade of his verandah while things rose up off the salt before us. We laughed at every shimmering mirage in shared disbelief. The priest said he hadn't touched a drop in fifteen years, that he'd gotten beyond magical thinking. But the salt lake kept him on his toes. And I saw what he meant. It was full of surprises.

I didn't exactly pull myself together – I got past such notions – but bits of me did come around again, as flies or memories or subatomic particles will for reasons of their own. Bit by bit I congregated, I suppose you could say, and then somehow I cohered. I went on and had another life. Or went ahead and made the best of the old one.

For a good while I feared excitement. But I found ways through that. I discovered something I was good at, something I could make my own. I am hell's own paramedic. When the shit hits the fan, I'm on, and people are glad to see me. They see the uniform and trust me, and that makes me happy. And it's all go, all adrenaline, fast and filthy.

When the girls were in school I stayed around for weekends and annual leave but now they're older I travel more. I go to wild places to surf or raft or hike. I've surfed over sunken warplanes in New Guinea and caught waves on the beach where Ollie North's bandits landed weapons. I've met plenty of nice people, men and women.

I suppose I'm celibate, which sounds kind of high-minded but it's been mostly a process of learning to make do. Which is a bit like married life, from what people tell me.

At the 2002 Winter Olympics an Australian aerial skier won a gold medal and became a national hero overnight to a largely snowless country. Suddenly she was all over the TV, this pretty blonde kid, spruiking for cereal and gum and God-knows-what. I thought of Eva.

More recently I was in an airport lounge where oppressively large video screens showed highlights from the winter games in Turin. For ten minutes or so we had to watch replays of an aerial skier coming unstuck. The high, twisting trajectory. The quarter rotation too far. You could see the brute fact of her ruined knee as she landed. We got close-ups to confirm it, and there was something ghoulishly excitable about the commentary intoned over the footage as it played time and again. Passengers around me barely stirred. They were tired and this highwire ski stuff was old hat already. Yet there she was, this girl, careering down the mountain on her back in a scouring spray, trying to hold her leg together. Howling. Over and again. It was as if she might be forced to spend eternity doing nothing else but skitter, failed and lame, downhill. I had to get up with my bags and move away, take myself through the miserable repeated franchises of the terminal in an effort to stay calm. It wasn't Eva this nightmare repetition reminded me of – it was the memory of my former self – and the slow-motion replay an illustration of how my mind had worked for too long.

Apparently there is nothing to fear in life but fear itself. This is the sort of shit you hear in the pub or at handover at the ambulance depot. Much talk about fear, as it happens. Along with chat about celebrities and weight loss and the award rate.

Most people don't like being afraid. You can hardly blame them. Thriving on risk is perverse – unless you're in business. Entrepreneurs are valiant but BASE jumpers are reckless fools. Solo sailors are a waste of rescue resources and snowboarders who leap from helicopters are suicidal showponies. War correspondents, as we all know, are creeps. Some risks, it would seem, are beyond respecting. Meanwhile nearly everyone is terrified that *this*, whatever life has become, is *it*. And what's worse is, it'll be over soon. That kind of fear – like toothache – can be accommodated. Well, most of the time.

Such is the sort of thing I mull over in my corner of the crib room while the youngsters are watching Idol and texting their loved ones. It's how I fill the time when nothing's happening. Thinking too much, flirting with melancholy.

But the moment a call comes, I'm up and out, laughing, afraid – and happy as a dog with two dicks.

The received wisdom in our game is that paramedics are either angels or cowboys and apparently I'm the last living example of the latter. Mostly I'm not offended. The people I work with and work on have either been mad or are going mad, so I usually feel at home.

I do a good job. When the siren's wailing I'm fully present; I am the best of me. I'm charged to the eyelids yet inside there's a still, quiet place like the middle of a cyclone. I like the priestly authority of the uniform, vehicle and lights, the reassurance they offer people as we arrive. When punters see the tunic and the resus bag they calm down a little and find faith and while I work, my faith meets theirs. I'm there to save, to improve the odds, to make good.

You win some jobs and you lose others.

There are nights like last night when you're always going to be too late, where you're just holding people's hands. I tried not to take it personally but it set me back, that call-out to the burbs. Just a rush of wind from the past, like a window momentarily slid aside. I know the difference between teenage suicide and a fatal abundance of confidence. I know what a boy looks like when he's strangled himself for fun.

I blow the didj until it hurts, until my lips are numb, until some old lady across the way gives me the finger.

A FEW WEEKS of the year I drive south to Sawyer with the honest intention of fixing up the old house. The mill is gone and the cow paddocks are planted with vines. The town is all wineries and bed-and-breakfast joints.

A couple of lesbians make cheese on the property next door. They're like a comedy routine, The Two Ronnies, and they're good neighbours.

I don't see anyone I used to know, except Slipper from the Angelus crew who's bald and paddles a surfski out at the Point some days. Sando and Eva's place is gone and the property has been subdivided. Lawyers and architects from the city have built ostentatious weekenders all over it.

The old Brewer is still in Dad's shed. It's not been ridden since the day I lost it at Old Smoky. Nowadays out there at the bommie, surfers have themselves towed into the wave with jetskis. You can only imagine the noise and the stink of petrol. Barney's is still surfed but not often. The resident great white seems to linger, and now he has protected status as an endangered species. As far as I know, the Nautilus remains undiscovered by the new generation.

I never actually get around to doing much to the house when I'm down in Sawyer. Time's too precious. I have an old ten-footer, a real clunker from the sixties, like something Gidget would ride. I shove it into the ute, drive down to the Point and paddle it out through the knots of scab-nosed bodyboarders to pick off a wave from every second set.

I'm not there to prove anything – I'm nearly fifty years old. I've got arthritis and a dud shoulder. But I can still maintain a bit of style. I slide down the long green walls into the bay to feel what I started out with, what I lost so quickly and for so long: the sweet momentum, the turning force underfoot, and those brief, rare moments of grace. I'm dancing, the way I saw blokes dance down the line forty years ago.

My girls stay with me now and then. Sometimes they bring their blokes; I don't mind so much. I tidy the house for a week before they arrive. They've seen chaos at first hand so they value order. My job reassures them, I think, lets them see I have a purpose in the world. The work and their interest help me manage myself. I toil at it. For them it's been important to know I'm not useless. I think they understand how tough the gig is, that I save lives and try to be kind. I've done my best to explain my troubles without resorting to indelicacy. They're adults now yet I'm still vigilant, careful not to startle, because there's been so much damage, too much shame.

My favourite time is when we're all at the Point, because when they see me out on the water I don't have to be cautious and I'm never ashamed. Out there I'm free. I don't require management. They probably don't understand this, but it's important for me to show them that their father is a man who dances – who saves lives and carries the wounded, yes, but who also does something completely pointless and beautiful, and in this at least he should need no explanation.